IN DEFIANCE
OF APARTHEID

"For evil can be forgiven but not forgotten."

ELIO ZANNONI

African Perspectives Publishing
PO Box 95342, Grant Park 2051,
Johannesburg, South Africa
www.africanperspectives.co.za

ISBN PRINT: 978-1-0370-2165-7
ISBN DIGITAL: 978-1-0370-2271-5

Editor: Carine Hartman
Proofreader: Raphael d'Abdon
Typesetter: Phumzile Mondlani
Cover Design: Jenilee Prinsloo - Ryzenberg

Contents

Dedication

Dedicated to all those special people with whom I shared love, affection and genuine friendship during the course of my life.

Also, to the people of South Africa in the hope that no present or future generation will ever have to experience the evil of a repressive regime again.

A Word of Gratitude

A special word of gratitude to my niece Silvia for acting as my personal counsellor during my writing endeavours. Sincere appreciation also to Rose Francis, my publisher for her experienced guidance throughout.

Author's Note

By nature, I am rather reserved. It is not easy to share my experiences and emotions. Perhaps because age is creeping up on me, I feel I have to get 'out of my shell' and share a part of my life with you. Me, as a young man, experiencing independence in a strange country I now call home; out of my 'comfort zone', away from my family and the small provincial town in the Northern Italian province of Veneto where I grew up.

I could have chosen other countries, but opportunity led me to an unusual and remote place: South Africa. A country at the far end of the African continent, known for its gold and diamond resources and the famous 'world-first' heart transplant in 1967 by Professor Christiaan Barnard. But also – at least back in the '80s – known for its policies of racial segregation, summed up in a single word with a very distinctive Afrikaans sound: Apartheid.

In that environment I had unique experiences that profoundly transformed me on a personal and emotional level. They also helped me develop a strong sense of humanity, justice, freedom and respect for those we share our world and life with.

I hope my personal story will be a valuable learning tool. Yes, it is a story lived between the '80s and '90s, which has profound relevance today, where hatred and discrimination often infiltrate relationships. If you take one lesson from this book, I hope it is of sound values: never give up in the face of injustice and continue to follow the principles of tolerance and respect for human dignity and freedom. These should be the foundations of our common living.

Foreword

Elio Zannoni's story is one of emigration. Like myself, he is one of the millions of Northeastern Italians who left their motherland to create something different, empowering and new for themselves and their families. It does not matter whether this desire was fueled by sheer necessity, the search for love, money, success, or by an adventurous spirit: Elio's people, the *Veneti* (and mine, the *Friulani*), have historically been at the forefront of Italian emigration around the world and in South Africa.

Writing about emigration is an appeal to dig into the roots of one's history and shifting identity. In this autobiographical tale, the author has accepted the challenge to give voice to his life story: to experiences of separation and reunion, to events in which hope and disappointment, dreams and awakening, toil and success, sacrifice and goals are intertwined, offering testimony to what has been and continues to be his journey.

Readers regardless of nationality, language, age, or cultural background can relate to this story. They belong not only to those who, like me and him, have left their country, but also to those who have stayed behind and to those who, on the other side of the path, have welcomed us in our new home. They belong to all of us, to this enigmatic, miraculous, unique human puzzle called South Africa.

Like all autobiographical narratives, this book was born from the desire to bring to the fore events that too often remain confined behind the scenes. For the writer this is always a healing process. In this text, the readers are invited to embark on a curative, transformative journey that if taken, will allow themselves to redefine their own borders, both physical and imaginary. We all know that life is a journey, but a book such as this, exuding compassion and empathy, reminds us that every journey becomes more fruitful, restorative and intense when shared.

There are feelings of detachment and separation in these pages, as well as dreams and fears of a life that constantly reinvents itself. Elio shares his hopes and recalls the defeats, the suffering, the disappointments encountered and the multiple occasions when he reached rock bottom and had to start all over again when the only thing he could count on was his inner strength and stubbornness.

Raphael d'Abdon, Pretoria, 9 March 2025

South Africa on the map

It was a sweltering Italian summer in 1982 when the letter from South Africa landed in my lap with an unexpected and exciting opportunity. I had just obtained a diploma in Classics, studying the civilisations of ancient Rome and Greece at the Liceo Classico, a school in my birthplace, Montebelluna, a small town near Venice, which – unlike the city of love – had a homogeneous society and virtually no foreigners.

Sitting at my study desk on that hot day, I was listening to the sounds of the doves and cicadas screeching in the heat, bored with no new studies or work prospects on the horizon. But it was a care-free time with friends and girlfriends enjoying each other's company in the cafés and piazzas without any worry: that would come later.

As a black belt, first dan from the age of 16, I taught judo to an all-female class at a local dojo for some pocket money. I was not in a steady relationship, but I think Cupid had struck the heart of a young girl who happened to be in the same dojo as me. I was very fit, with an adventurous mind, ready to grab new opportunities.

I came from a hard-working family of food traders. My father, Claudio, was the oldest of four brothers all working in the same family business – a grocery store and a wholesale distribution centre. Having seen their frequent squabbles, I could not agree more with the Italian proverb, *'Amore di Fratelli, amore di coltelli'* ('Love of brothers, love of knives'), which described the conflict amongst close family members who happen to run a business together.

My mother, Bruna, was a typical Italian housewife, committed to her kids' well-being. She was – at least in her younger days – an attractive woman with blonde hair and green eyes. I still think of her as a typical example of how true diplomats should be, caring for others and avoiding or solving interpersonal conflict at all costs.

My father was a good, gentle man who did not shy away from his emotional side. He had some distinctive Italian looks and habits, with dark hair neatly combed back with perfumed gel, and incredibly blue eyes.

Time had left its mark on their appearance. I definitely inherited my mother's diplomatic side – and probably her looks too – and believe it or not, my father's true Italian emotions. The two, with great sacrifice, instilled in all of us high moral standards.

My sister, Franca, is nine years older than me. Married, she had already experienced the excitement of travelling; first to Spain, where her husband lived as an expat working in the high fashion industry, then to South Africa, where the sparkle of diamonds had lured him to the precious stones trade in Johannesburg - a city known by many names: Joburg; the City of Gold; iGoli in isiZulu, the language spoken by a local ethnic group and Goudstad in Afrikaans.

Afrikaans as a language developed in the 17th and 18th centuries from Dutch spoken by European colonists, enslaved people, and indigenous Khoisan in the Dutch Cape Colony. It also incorporates influences from Malay, Portuguese, Indonesian, and the Khoekhoe and San languages. Also known as the *'kombuistaal'* or 'kitchen language', it is spoken by the Afrikaners, called 'Boers' or 'farmers' who, at the time of my arrival, were solidly at the helm of the government of the *Republiek van Suid Afrika.*

Franca and I got on well. She was caring with an acute, inquisitive mind; always ready to ask pertinent questions. While in Italy, she had embarked upon the study of psychology at a local university. When she left for South Africa to join her husband, she had just given birth to my niece, Silvia, a cute, chubby baby, blonder than Germans, and full of life. So, Franca became a dedicated mother and wife, leaving her study and career aspirations behind.

Like many little boys, a uniform sent my imagination racing. I dreamt of wearing a police uniform or a sheriff hat and was always carrying toy guns. Crime fighting seemed a natural career choice, so I started thinking of registering for a university degree in crime-related studies. The question was where? And at which university?

And that is when a letter from South Africa changed my life. The envelope had a stamp from Joburg, a faraway place so remote I only knew it existed because Franca had recently moved there. The pages were filled with fresh news I knew I had to share with my parents – but the last couple of paragraphs had my heart beating faster.

While searching for courses to study, my brother-in-law, Roberto (Robi), had come across an interesting degree in Police Science, offered by the Department of Criminology at the University of South Africa, based in Pretoria, the capital city of the country. This course, Franca wrote, seemed to fit me like a glove.

I pondered on it for days. I could study the subject of my dreams, but it meant I had to leave everything behind: my parents; my safe haven; my friends and, last but not least, my country.

What can I expect from a country located on the other side of the world, 8 000km from home, a foreign land, known for Apartheid and its policies of racial segregation under laws introduced in 1948?

And what about that foreign concept of that single stern word, 'Apartheid'? I knew it was an Afrikaans term meaning 'apartness' or 'the state of being separate', but little else, except what Franca told me in her letters: Blacks and people of colour, such as Indians, Asians and South Africa's unique mixed-blood group, the Coloureds, were forced to live apart from Whites.

I found my answer. Dreams are bigger than concepts. I'm going. I was ready for a new chapter in my young life – I bought a ticket.

I had never been on an intercontinental flight before. Carrying heavy hand luggage filled with memories I could not possibly leave behind, I knew this was a drastic change in my life. No more comforts - just the unknown.

I boarded Alitalia's *Tintoretto* in Rome, unprepared for the stopover in Nairobi, Kenya, before landing in Johannesburg.

It was a long night flight, with me staring out of the window into total darkness, with only a few faint lights illuminating the Sahara Desert. Who can live in such isolation, I wondered.

Then I met Africa. Night made way for the indescribable light of the rising African sun.

The air looked fresh, pure and unpolluted, so radiant and cloudless, unlike the Venetian skies I was accustomed to. The continent, seen from 10 000m above sea level, appeared untouched and vast with free-flowing rivers and immense lakes. My mind ran rampant with images of animals wandering freely in the sanctity of their natural habitat.

I did not share any of this with my fellow-passenger, a good looking, petite, dark-haired Italian girl named Aurora. She was on her way to see family members in a town near Joburg, called Germiston, known for its gold mines and refinery.

"Nice name," I said as an icebreaker. "What will you be doing in Germiston?"

"It's just a vacation. I'll be there for a short time. You?"

"I'll be staying in South Africa for quite some time, I think. I'm going to register as a student of Police Science and Criminology at a local university."

That got her going: "Really exciting! I hope I'll also have an opportunity to study abroad one day. Rome, where I live, is a fascinating city but it's getting too small for my ambitions."

I just had to take her number.

About an hour from landing, Joburg was in my face. The isolated, sparsely populated land I became accustomed to during the flight now showed increased urbanisation, advanced infrastructure with highways and roads crossing each other, bridges and industrial areas. Then another view also caught my eye - endless rows of tiny houses that looked the same. I learnt later that Black and Coloured working classes living in poverty in townships on the margins of society call them home.

This was in great contrast to the neatly organised suburbs where middle-class and affluent Whites lived. I had never seen so many crystal-blue swimming pools.

Just before we landed, I saw shining golden hills on the horizon. "What can that be?" I asked a South African passenger sitting in my row.

"You're in the land of gold, my friend. Those are huge mine dumps that stand as monuments to what was once the largest gold mining area in the world, dating back to 1886."

The plane's wheels thumped on the tarmac. I realised my journey had begun.

"Welcome to South Africa" said an attractive lady in Italian whilst leaning over my seat wearing bright red lipstick.

"Am I famous?" I asked myself.

"Please follow me," she said with a gorgeous smile. I had just met Tizi, an Alitalia ground hostess and wife-to-be of Robi's brother, Massimo (Max), the same Max she tells me will be my "driver".

Known for his sense of humour and vibrant lifestyle, I could not have wished for a better escort. "What a welcome," I thought.

Travelling along a highway one would see in any American city – not at all what I imagined an African road would look like – I spotted a huge square complex. "That's a shopping centre," Max said. "There are many like that in Joburg - big enough to get lost inside while shopping!"

Travelling up a hill, I remembered the Montello hill my friends and I climbed in many of our excursions when Max said: "This is Sylvia's Pass, one of the many steep inclines in the city with an altitude of almost 2 000m."

The name "Sylvia" immediately reminded me of my little niece who shared the same name. I will hug her and Franca soon, I thought.

I spotted many homes with the Italian flag flying outside. "We're in Orange Grove, also known as 'Little Italy', because many Italians live here. There are also a few places that serve a good cappuccino," Max explained.

We passed through Norwood, a suburb with a continental feel of restaurants and shops on each side of the road. I could not have known then that Norwood would soon become the place where I would spend most of my free time.

With Max's convertible roof down, I felt the clean African breeze as my long hair flew in all directions. The sun was high in the bluest sky I had ever seen. I could feel it warming my skin; intense rays lulling me as I struggled to keep my eyes open. I was in a new land, where the forces of nature were much more powerful than back home. I whipped out my sunglasses and since that day, they became a distinctive feature of my appearance. Either wearing them or resting them on top of my head as if they were an extension of my body.

We finally arrived at Sanlam Park, a residential complex not far from Norwood where Franca and Robi lived with little Silvia. Max lived in the same complex, so the family reunion helped to cushion – at least initially – the drastic changes lying ahead.

We were staying in a townhouse apartment of a complex where all units looked the same and were painted the colour of their residents - white. The only Black people there were either working as domestic workers or employed by management as gardeners and handymen. Robi and Max were very busy with their new business venture as diamond and precious stone dealers at an office in Noord Street, downtown Joburg. Franca spent most of her time looking after Silvia and doing what a typical Italian housewife does - prepare wonderful dishes.

I had no car and no friends, and was in "idle mode", wandering around the complex and sometimes crossing the road to visit the local shopping mall. The communal swimming pool was a favourite as I could lie in the African sun admiring the beauty of the local women, many with fair skin and long blonde hair, clearly of English, Dutch, German and French Huguenot descent. But where were the women of other skin colours hiding? Robi had the answer: "Don't forget you're in Apartheid country. They're not allowed to live in this complex and could never make use of this swimming pool. It's reserved for the exclusive use of White persons."

"Ah, of course, Apartheid, racial segregation - Whites with Whites, Blacks with Blacks" I reminded myself.

To break my daily routine, I would go for a refreshing walk around the complex, thinking about the girlfriends I had left behind. I missed them and I missed not having new friends, especially female ones. I could hear the distinctive cooing of doves in very tall trees, singing as if they were accompanying me on my walks. I will always associate that sound with South Africa. Like the smell of guavas and intense lightning from powerful storms breaking the serenity of the African skies during summer; a fantastic manifestation of the power of nature - one of my favourite spectacles to watch.

Occasionally, I would walk all the way to Grant Avenue in Norwood, just for the sake of seeing a bit of city life and some window shopping. It was nice, but very different from the sophisticated and fashionable shop windows I was accustomed to in Italy!

Sometimes on Sundays, we visited Tizi, "my personal airport hostess" and her family in a suburb called Bramley, and spent the whole day around the swimming pool, listening to music. I remember the unmistakable beat of *Eye of the Tiger*, the hit of the moment, and Tizi and her sisters dancing and singing for us while we waited impatiently for the succulent meat and boerewors skilfully prepared by Max and Robi at the braai stand.

This weekend break with routine was welcomed, as Sundays were particularly boring due to some Apartheid law that forced businesses to remain closed from Saturday lunch time until Monday morning. This closure created not only a loss to the economy but also inconvenience. Grocery stores and fuel stations were closed, as well as places of entertainment such as cinemas and clubs. Liquor stores were also not allowed to operate, which forced many to stock up on liquor or resort to illegal trade. Black and Coloured townships, saw an increase in informal drinking establishments, commonly known as "shebeens", which operated without the required licence on the weekends.

"What kind of place is this? It's like America's Prohibition in the 1920s, when the infamous Italian American gangster Al Capone amassed an extraordinary fortune illegally. "How can the authorities dictate how and when people should be entertained?" I often asked myself.

The government's decision to control and restrict certain businesses and social activities on weekends was motivated by some biblical interpretation of Christianity, expressed by the Dutch Reformed Church, a dogma dominant among Afrikaners. Because of its support of racial discrimination, the church was expelled from the World Alliance of Reformed Churches in 1982, which declared Apartheid a sin. However, it was readmitted in the late '80s, when it changed its stance on Apartheid and opened its doors to all people.[1]

This conservative church, which openly supported Apartheid policies as if it were God's will, had devoted followers among the members of the "Nasionale Party" (National Party). At the time, the government was run by the famous (or rather infamous) PW Botha as "Eerste Minister" (Prime Minister), Magnus Malan, heading up "Verdediging" (Defence) and Pik Botha "Buitelandse Sake" (Foreign Affairs), just to name a few.

Tizi's suburb, Bramley, was a stone's throw from a large township and informal settlement called

Alexandra, where some of the Black population lived in hardship without access to basic human needs such as proper ablution facilities, water, electricity, and struggled to put together three meals a day. I was told it was not possible to go to Alexandra because it was dangerous for Whites. People of my skin colour were not welcome in that densely populated area. I made up my mind to visit one of these "no-go" townships one day. "Are they really as bad as they say they are?" I thought to myself.

On board the Apartheid train

Having made no new friends, I decided to try my luck with Aurora, the girl I had met on the plane. I dialled the number she gave me; *"Ciao come stai?"* - "How're you?" I asked.

"It's you! I was just thinking of you!" she replied. "There's a birthday party at my home tomorrow. Would you like to join us?"

"Well, it would be nice, but I've no car and don't even know where Germiston is!" But my spirit of adventure prevailed, and I ended the call with: "Don't worry! I'll make a plan. Just give me the address and I'll be there."

That is how I landed at Joburg Central Railway Station. I would simply take a train to Germiston.

"Are you sure? You don't know your way around yet," Robi reminded me before dropping me off. "No worries, I'll be perfectly fine," and off I went to the ticket desk and the platform I had been directed to. While waiting for the train, I was once again confronted with race segregation except now I was experiencing it first-hand. There were benches for "Whites Only" and "Non-Whites Only".

The train arrived and once again, I experienced Apartheid. The privilege of sitting in a first-class coach was reserved for passengers of my skin colour, while non-Whites had to travel in third-class coaches. Later, the locals explained that the segregation of public premises, vehicles and services was legalised by the Apartheid Law: "The Reservation of Separate Amenities Act of 1953". Only public roads and streets were excluded from the Act. Travelling for the first time by train made me reflect further on the race segregation policies in place in South Africa, all the way to the Germiston Railway Station where Aurora was waiting.

Aurora was excited to reconnect and, by the look of things, had already made some friends with local White youths who had also been invited to her party. I really felt like a foreigner as my English was not good at the time and Afrikaans was to me, just another language of the Babel Tower. Besides, they looked and behaved so differently from the friends I had left behind in Italy. Even the Italians born in South Africa had different ways and spoke an amusing Anglo-Italian language. "Dangerous", for example, became "Dangeroso" and "to park" was translated to "parkare". They were probably laughing at me when I was speaking my elementary English with an accent that was very strong at the time, although it has improved over the years. I was a fish out of water at this Whites-only party, in which the only Black person was the domestic worker who helped Aurora clean up our mess.

I saw Aurora once more before she returned to Italy. We spent a lovely afternoon at Zoo Lake, one of the many recreational parks in Joburg, located near a suburb called Forest Town, with one of the largest man-made aggregation of trees in the world. Interestingly Zoo Lake, due to some acquisition requirements, had been excluded from the Apartheid segregation policies, which meant it was accessible for all races.

Joburg's suburbs were well-organised, clean and well-maintained. The roads were in excellent conditions with no potholes in sight. When blooming, rows of jacaranda trees welcomed travellers with a beautiful carpet of purple flowers. While Norwood could generally be described as a middle-class suburb, some neighbouring suburbs, such as Houghton, were clearly upper-class, characterised by opulent properties large enough to potentially accommodate more than one family.

I was clearly a witness to the extreme riches of Joburg, predominantly in the hands of White elites – but the city also had well-developed commercial and industrial sectors run by non-Whites, especially of Asian (Indian and Lebanese) origin, as well as English and European immigrants such as Greeks, Germans, Portuguese, and Italians.

The living standards of the Whites were very high, even higher than those of people living in continental Europe and America. The cost of living was low, with affordable food, fuel, property ownership and rentals. The rand was strong against international currencies: R1 could buy 1 US dollar and many Italian lire.

When travelling through the affluent northern suburbs, I could see two distinctive landmarks. The Hillbrow Tower, at 270m probably one of the highest towers in Africa, and the cylindrical 55-storey Ponte City building in Berea. I heard about the great vibe of Hillbrow, a suburb just outside of the city centre, with one of the highest urban population densities in the southern hemisphere. It had a bustling city life, with plenty of cafés, restaurants, pizzerias, shops, clubs, and even some dodgy sex establishments. The latter were apparently not affected by the tight controls the Apartheid government had introduced with the Immorality Act of 1950.

I "met" Hillbrow through Bruno, a South African with Italian roots who owned an Alfa Romeo Junior. He was a racing maniac, who would make you fear for your life. I remember going up Louis Botha Avenue at an incredible speed and, in a flash, we were in Hillbrow.

Being accustomed to the old, historical and rather flat Italian architecture, the place was decidedly not Africa. I felt like I was in the United States with tall buildings on both sides of the street. We drove toward Pretoria Street, passing what looked like a strip club – The Summit Club. Loads of people were walking around. The majority White – but I also noticed other racial groups.

Bruno showed me the High Point shopping and residential complex, the Goblet disco club, Café Zurich, Café de Paris and Café Wien, and the very busy Pizzeria Romana, places where people could eat, drink and be merry. We passed the Bella Napoli, another disco club and stopped for a cappuccino at Mirella's, an Italian coffee shop overlooking Pretoria Street. What impressed me most was the busy, yet orderly city life unfolding before my eyes. "Yeah, I like Hillbrow! I'll be back." Little did I know I would become one of its staunchest residents.

Joburg central business district (CBD) had its own surprises. Robi's office in Noord Street was not far from a famous restaurant-cum-coffee bar called Rugantino, where I had countless espressos and cappuccinos, the exclusive Villa Borghese restaurant, the fancy Landdrost hotel and a typical pizzeria with the unmistakable Italian name 'Il Padrino' ('The Godfather') were also located nearby. I was amazed at the development. Buildings such as the Sanlam Centre and The Carlton Centre were stretching my neck backward to a point where I felt pain. Yes, I saw people of all races – but mainly Whites. I walked past many clubs, including Q's, where I later spent many late nights enjoying my favourite '80s disco music. Some historical buildings dated back to the beginnings of Joburg's golden days at the dawn of the 1900s, others were modern – signs that I was walking the streets of a young and vibrant city.

When Franca one Friday went to a downtown cinema with her friend, I was pleased to join them. We parked close to the venue in Troye Street, an area where nowadays you would run the risk of being attacked as you drive through, never mind walking. But then we were perfectly safe in an all-White cinema. We enjoyed the movie even though the fast American accents of the actors drove Franca and I crazy. Some scenes also appeared to have been cut. Later I learnt about the Apartheid regime's strict censorship through the Publication and Entertainment Act of 1963. South Africa had one of the most exhaustive film and publication censorship in the Western world, with thousands of films being studied, often frame by frame, and cut for scenes containing nudity, vulgar language and political issues that could be interpreted as being hostile to the government.

Going downtown soon became one of my passions. I knew every single street, corner, alley, establishment and, of course, coffee shop. I often used bus number 10 travelling from Norwood to the CBD via Hillbrow's Edith Cavell Street. I preferred bus rides, as they were relaxing and allowed me to observe the surroundings, including the "South African beauties" embellishing the lively city streets. Needless to say, there were no people of colour in these "Whites Only" buses. They had their own bus stops, stations and "Blacks Only" buses, run by Putco (Public Utility Transportation Corporation), which, since 1971, was owned by a powerful Italian family. Putco became the main "Blacks Only" bus transportation company in Joburg and, because it was seen as a symbol of oppression, it was frequently targeted with attacks and boycott actions.[2] "What kind of a place is this? Separate benches, separate train coaches, separate buses, separate housing, separate ablutions, separate lives."

Close encounters of an Apartheid kind

I always felt safe walking in downtown Joburg. The locals told me the reason for this was the Apartheid government's strict application of law and order which kept the public feeling secure. True, although this applied mostly to areas where Whites lived and worked. Being White did not mean that you could do as you pleased. The then "Suid Afrikaanse Polisie" (SAP or South African Police) was a well-organised, no-nonsense force. It was not a service as it was re-branded in 1994 as the South African Police Service or SAPS. No, the SAP was feared by all; Whites and non-Whites, but particularly the latter, often being the recipients of excessive and, at times, unjustifiably brutal force. They fought crime but also repressed anti-government demonstrations and upheld Apartheid laws.

The police were an extension of the Apartheid state – more specifically of the National Party's authority over people and therefore, were not independent from political interference. The Nationalist Party, who governed from 1948 to 1994 before it was disbanded in 2005, promoted Afrikaner interest and culture, strongly upholding Apartheid policies and White domination. The SAP protected the White minority government of the day, rather than the citizens. Controlling Black South Africans was part of their mandate.[3]

For many, the symbol of that repression was a tall, cold building, looking towards the highway in an almost menacing way - John Vorster Square. Named after John Vorster, Prime Minister from 1966 to 1978, it was home to the much-feared Johannesburg Security Branch. Now known as Johannesburg Central Police Station, its 9th and 10th floors were the place where the Security Police conducted brutal interrogations on anti-Apartheid activists in special sound-proof rooms, designed for the purposes of "getting people to talk". Some activists died in their custody; others "committed suicide" by jumping from the top floor of the building. At least seven people died between 1971 and 1990 while held indefinitely under Apartheid detention laws[4], most notably activist Steve Biko, whose death in 1977 caused widespread protests and international condemnation and sanctions, isolating South Africa from the rest of the world. Other people were eliminated, some never to be found, by Vlakplaas (meaning "flat farm" in Afrikaans from the location where it was based). Also known as section C1 and later C10, Vlakplaas was an undercover counterinsurgency unit that operated in the '80s under the control of the police Security Branch. Its mission was to go after the opponents of the Apartheid state to either convert or execute them.

Those converted would become Askaris ("soldiers") and infiltrate the Black community as spies.

Though the powerful SAP was well in control of White officers at management level, it was – ironically – from the early '80s forced to start recruiting from the non-White population, as many officers had left the force for better paid jobs in the private security sector. The working conditions and power of the so-called instant constables (kitskonstabels in Afrikaans) fell far short of that afforded to their White counterparts. They received less training, lower salaries and, with a few exceptions, they were not allowed to carry firearms. They could only use batons, sjamboks (a stiff whip made of rhinoceros hide) and knobkerries (a short stick with a big head). They were mainly given foot patrol and riot control duties in the townships where the Apartheid government had difficulty maintaining law and order.[5]

For that, they paid an even higher price. Many instant constables were considered "traitors" or "sell outs" for joining the White regime's police force and were brutally killed by members of their communities.

The real pillars of Apartheid were the draconian security laws passed to segregate and intimidate those who dared to oppose the authorities. One of the most extreme laws – amongst others – was passed under Vorster's leadership; the Terrorism Act of 1967 allowed the police to detain, indefinitely and in solitary confinement, anyone suspected of "terrorism", defined as "anyone who might endanger the maintenance of law and order", or "having information about terrorism". No court could intervene, and no one had access to the detainees.[6]

I recall seeing the police stopping Black people at random and, after a brief interaction, loading them into the back of their van. "Why are they doing that?" I asked a South African friend. "They're asking them to produce their 'passbook', a sort of internal passport; and if they don't have it with correct information regarding their identity, area of residence and employment, they're arrested, taken to a police station and eventually to court."

That is how I learnt about the infamous "Pass Law". The Apartheid regime in 1952 passed this law, making it compulsory for every Black person from the age of 16 to always carry a Passbook when they travelled inside urban areas considered "restricted to Whites". Colloquially, passes were often called the *dompas*, literally meaning the "stupid pass" – or perhaps just a syllabic abbreviation for "domestic passport".

"But they're native to this country!" I replied. Obviously not for the regime. Apart from the implementation of strict controls on the movement of non-Whites – Blacks in particular, they also relocated them according to their ethnic identity, to respective independent and self-governing homelands, or Bantustans. Gazankulu, KwaZulu, Lebowa, KwaNdebele, KaNgwane, Qwaqwa, Transkei, Bophuthatswana, Venda and Ciskei – all territories created by the architects of Apartheid in 1950, with Hendrik Verwoerd (Minister of Native Affairs) in a leading role.

These unjust laws were met with protests between the '50s and early '60s, passive resistance and the burning of passbooks. Then came the 21st of March 1960. In the township of Sharpeville near Vereeniging, the police opened fire on a crowd of approximately 5 000 people gathered in response to a call made by the Pan-Africanist Congress (PAC), a liberation movement formed in 1959. The PAC had asked Black people to leave their passbooks at home and demanded the police arrest them for contravening the Pass laws.

The police fired over 1000 rounds into the crowd, in what is known as the Sharpeville Massacre. For more than 50 years, the number of people killed and injured has been based on the police record, which included 249 victims in total, including 29 children, with 69 people killed and 180 injured. Recent research has shown at least 91 people were killed at

Sharpeville and 238 people wounded. Many people were shot in the back as they fled from the police.[7] There was no doubt the Apartheid state was powerful, well-organised and equipped for domination.

It had also launched a programme for the research and development of weapons of mass destruction, which led to the construction of the first nuclear weapons in 1982. According to the Nuclear Threat Initiative, it had also used anthrax and botulinum toxin to target perceived enemies of the regime. However, in 1993, with the end of Apartheid and close to the first democratic elections, this programme was dismantled when South Africa joined the Non-Proliferation Treaty as a non-nuclear state.[8]

One day, walking alone in downtown Joburg, I noticed a pretty lady approaching. She was Coloured - of a mixed race with long, straight, shining black hair. I admired her, despite the red lights flashing in the back of my head warning me of the Apartheid laws. Specifically, the Immorality Amendment Act of 1950, first introduced in 1927, that made it a criminal offence for people of different races to have sexual relationships – not only between Whites and Blacks, but also between Whites and Coloured or Indian and Asian people.

Allow me to digress: the Apartheid government had classified citizens in four main racial groups: "White", "Coloured" (mixed race), "Indian" (Asian) and "Black" (natives), with the first having the highest status, followed by the second and third and, of course, last the Black Africans. As if prohibiting sex between people of different races was not enough, the state also interfered with the rights of lovers wanting to get married, no matter the colour of the skin, with the introduction of the Prohibition of Mixed Marriages Act of 1949. "What kind of racially defined morality is this? To dictate to people who they could have sex with or whom they marry?" I was baffled.

The Italian in me ignored those red flags. "I can't let her pass without trying my luck!" I simply asked her how she was; "Hello, how're you?" She looked at me in disbelief. Who is this White guy approaching her in such a direct manner? She stopped.

I can't remember what I said to her in my broken English, but I was able to write down my name and home number on a piece of paper, hoping she would call me.

And she did!

An amused Franca told me there was an English-speaking girl asking for me. Carol – that was her name. She asked whether I was still interested in seeing her again. "Sure! Where should we hook up?"

"You need to come to Joubert Park, near the Hillbrow Hospital, where I stay." I somehow managed to write down her address and we had a date.

Bruno and his speedy Alfa Romeo came to the rescue again. "You're crazy!" he said. "That's not a safe location, with all those Coloured people living in those flats; you're looking for trouble!" He dropped me off in front of this "really dodgy" building, according to Bruno, but I was not worried as I knew I had to see this girl again.

Walking to the entrance, I noticed most people living there were Coloureds and Indians. Obviously, the segregation laws imposed by the Group Areas Act of 1950 which effectively excluded people of colour from living in areas reserved for Whites had been somewhat relaxed in Hillbrow.

I was a bit uneasy as I pulled the building's screeching entrance door open and walked up the stairs, crossing paths with some residents who looked rather surprised to see me there. I was nervous when I knocked on Carol's door – but not as nervous as she was. She flung open the door with a "Please come in quickly! I don't want other people to see me with a White guy!"

Once inside, she told me she was home alone as her sister had gone out with friends. "Lucky me," I thought – until the door swung open not long after and I was faced with her very unfriendly sister and friends.

I tried to shake one guy's hand, but he ignored that, telling me I was not welcome. I could hear Carol's sister shouting, telling her she was stupid to bring a White guy to the flat as it could cause problems with the landlord because other residents would not hesitate to spy on them. That is when Carol showed me the door.

At that moment, I felt the coldness of Apartheid and understood its negative impact on relationships between people of different races. I found myself "lost" in a dark street in Hillbrow, having been booted out by my new-found "girlfriend". And now I may be attacked by some bad elements who do not approve of my presence and the colour of my skin. Then I heard the distinctive noise of an Alfa Romeo engine. It was Bruno, coming to the rescue. "I warned you so!" was his first comment when I told him what had just happened. "We're not in Italy. We've Apartheid in this country! It's dangerous to mix with 'these' people! Stay clear or the authorities will ship you back to Italy!"

Unlike Luca a friend of the family, who came to South Africa to find new opportunities. He was older, with a different personality. He was much more of a social person who liked a good glass of wine. Whilst socialising was not for him, one evening, having borrowed Robi's car, I asked him to accompany me downtown for an evening of relaxation. We ended up at the Rand International Hotel in Bree Street, where people of different races were known to get together away from the long arm of the Apartheid laws.

Luca was rather shy with girls, and he kept to himself sipping on a double whiskey on the rocks. Two Coloured ladies, realising I was interested, did not waste time in moving over. Candice, the prettiest, told us about a party at a township called Eldorado Park – known as Eldos – and we were invited, provided they could get a lift. I had never heard of Eldos and therefore did not know the directions. I did know a township was a place where people of a specific racial group, segregated under the Group Areas Act, lived. In fact, Eldos was established in the mid-1960s and declared an area for the exclusive settlement of Coloured people.

We kept on driving for almost half an hour, with me not having a clue where we were going. "Could we trust these girls? Are they taking us to a trap where some criminals will rob us of the car, or even worse?"

The girls were reassuring, knowing that the longer we drove, the more nervous we all became. We were fully aware that, as Whites, if we were to encounter a police roadblock, we would have been in serious trouble for being at the "wrong" place in the company of the "wrong"' passengers.

It was already late as we drove through an area where houses and roads all looked the same, a sort of labyrinth. Suddenly, our hosts told us to park near a house where we could hear the deafening sound of disco music – a clear indication we had reached the party.

We were introduced as "friends from Italy" – and this Italian could not stop staring at some of the girls. They were pretty, albeit a bit rowdy, and they loved the unexpected guests. Some of the guys, instead, were suspicious of these two Whitey's rocking up at their party uninvited, accompanying local girls.

Candice insisted I should follow her to a nearby house. "Don't worry, come with me, I want you to see where I stay and meet my sisters," she said. Her place was modest, a typical small township house. "Please come and see my new Italian boyfriend!" she shouted at her sisters as we entered the living room. I was, I realised, a "trophy" to be shown off.

What I did not know while I was being paraded, was that the police were raiding the party venue searching for illegal activities and goods. Helped by his dark hair and complexion, the cops did not realise that Luca, a White guy, was among the crowd. Had I been there, instead of impressing

Candice's sisters, they would have immediately spotted me with my blonde hair and fair skin and probably taken me in for questioning.

It was time to go home – not an easy task when your passenger is asleep, and you have no idea how to escape the Eldos labyrinth. Finally, I saw a signboard with the word 'Johannesburg' pointing in a northerly direction. "At last, we made it out of Eldos in one piece!" I told myself, while looking at the signboard as if it were Jesus with open arms showing me the way to salvation.

***

The big day – the purpose for me being in South Africa – finally arrived when Robi made time to accompany me to register for the degree of my choice in Police Science and Criminology at the Department of Criminology at the University of South Africa (Unisa), one of the largest universities in the country, where struggle icon Nelson Mandela also received his degree in Law.

I was finally about to study the subjects required for my dream career and was walking on air, feeling as if my life was about to become more exciting and purposeful.

We travelled to Pretoria on a scorching hot day. That city was always at least three degrees Celsius hotter than Joburg due to its lower altitude. Then I spotted a futuristic building, like an enormous transatlantic cruise ship, on top of a hill. "That's Unisa," Robi said. I could hardly believe I would be studying at such an amazing place. The Unisa Department of Criminology had acquired a prestigious reputation due to its commitment to advancing research and policy analysis on issues of public safety, criminal justice and crime. I remember the frequent interactions with brilliant lecturers who, knowing I was a foreign student – probably the only one from Europe at the time – guided and extended my understanding of the discipline I was studying. I was a proud Unisa student and worked diligently to achieve my degrees despite the initial language barrier.

My knowledge of English was basic, as I had completed only two years of this language at the Liceo Classico in Italy. In that school, we were forced to drop important subjects such as English and French, in favour of Latin and Ancient Greek, two "dead" languages that made us sweat blood and tears for a full five years. "But they certainly helped use your mind logically," some academics told me when we debated the usefulness of some ancient languages at the expense of those that could really help when travelling, studying and working abroad.

I decided to enrol in a course in English. The Language College was in downtown Joburg, in Bree

Street. The classes were a mix of people from different countries and walks of life, all of us speaking English with the most incredible accents. I remember being unable to stop myself from laughing when our Chinese classmate attempted to read from a textbook – not that my accent was any better. Even South Africa's natives sounded different when they spoke English. Black people had a distinctive accent, as did Indians, Coloureds and Whites, particularly those who spoke Afrikaans as a first language. While Whites and Coloureds were for the most part bilingual and spoke English and Afrikaans, Indians spoke predominantly English. Black people were multilingual as they could converse in a variety of languages: from English to native tongues such as isiZulu, Sepedi, Sesotho, Setswana and isiXhosa. Many could also communicate in Afrikaans but refused to speak it, as they considered it to be the language of the oppressors.

My experience travelling to Unisa in Pretoria – then a city mostly populated by Afrikaners – confirmed that it was almost an insult for Afrikaners to speak English and vice versa, because of their bloody colonial battles against the British in the Anglo-Boer war from 1899 to 1902. After the British had crushed the Boers' resistance, the war ended with the signing of the Peace Treaty of Vereeniging and the Boers' acceptance of British sovereignty with limited self-governing control.

What made hostilities between the two even worse was the full-scale repression by the British, who broke the spirit of the Boer guerilla units by capturing and herding the families of Boer soldiers into concentration camps.[9]

The Afrikaners' anti-British stand became even more evident when a referendum, held in 1960 to declare South Africa a Republic independent from Britain, was passed by the majority of the White electorate. Other racial groups were excluded from voting.

Afrikaners' hostility toward English-speaking people was probably attributable to the fact that the English were viewed as liberal and against Apartheid policies. It became a reality to me when I joined a parachutist club, north of Pretoria, where I did a crash course with some "psycho" instructors who made us jump from a small plane after only two hours of training. Before the jump, I approached a group of fellow trainees who, after they learnt I was from Joburg, in their heavy Afrikaans accent told me in no uncertain terms that they wanted nothing to do with people from Joburg. I was not welcome. Not only because of the animosity between Afrikaners and English speakers, but also because the level of conservatism between Pretoria and the more liberal Joburg differed.

On that day, I ended up at a Pretoria hospital with a dislocated shoulder, the result of a freak accident caused by the parachute static line catching my right arm as I jumped out of the plane. Being unable to manoeuvre the parachute and driven by an adrenaline rush in a surreal silence, I somehow managed to avoid a large tree as I rapidly descended and fell onto the harsh African soil with a loud thump. Fortunately, the main parachute had opened with only a few seconds to spare.

***

A Greek Cypriot I had met at the language school, Kyriacos, told me about a Unisa study centre downtown Joburg where students could study and borrow the books needed for their subjects. The library was inside a complex called the Tony Factor Centre, a small shopping centre in the heart of the city, between Rissik and Pritchard Street, named after a dyslexic entrepreneur who opened Downtown Furnishers in the '70s, with many others following countrywide. Factor was known as the "Discount King" and even sold cut-price coffins, turning his initial R900 investment into R1.4 billion.

It was there that I realised Unisa was a multi-racial university, with students of all colours and creeds silently absorbing the contents of their books, seemingly intent on making a better life for themselves. I felt comfortable in that multi-racial environment and soon after my first visit, became part of the library's furniture.

When I discovered an Italian bar, the Brazilian Coffee Shop, I was in my element. I was greeted by three middle-aged Italian ladies, who, when heard I was from Italy, peppered me with questions as if I was at John Vorster Square. Signora - Mrs Sartor, the most vocal of them, did not waste time to invite me for supper at her family home when she heard I was from Veneto province, a town close to her birthplace. I became one of the Brazilian Coffee Shop's best customers, loving their espressos, macchiatos and cappuccinos with the occasional toasted sandwich, when my finances would allow.

Discovering the Italian bookstore L'Edicola next door, my cup was truly running over. That is where I bought newspapers and magazines, devouring news from Italy and feeling a bit closer to home. The internet was still developing and not yet a daily reality. Letters were how I kept in touch with my faraway loved ones.

Life was great and I was happy – even happier to be studying in a multi-racial library with a melting pot of people and ideas; a place where different races and cultures were allowed to interact without the interference of security branch agents. They occasionally came to look for "hot-headed" individuals who could pose a threat to the government but never found them at the library.

Not that there were no 'hotheads' around, I thought as I looked around the library. On my right was Sam a Coloured man with strong political beliefs against Apartheid. He was studying Sociology. On my left was Sipho, a Black guy studying toward a Bachelor of Law degree. He was the most militant of the students and often tried to entice me into politically charged discussions. Maybe because of my rudimentary English or maybe because of the diplomatic approach I had learnt from my mother – I never debated with him.

Sitting a short distance away was Zolile, a student in Police Science and Criminology, the degree I had also registered for. He was fascinated by my neat handwriting and, being a gentle and respectful soul, one day he timidly asked me whether I could write some love sentences in English to his girlfriend! I was astonished but did it without further question.

Zolile was from Transkei, the place where former South African President and anti-Apartheid icon Nelson Mandela was born. Transkei was created by the Apartheid state in 1959 as one of 10 Bantustans and designated, together with Ciskei, for the Xhosa-speaking people of South Africa.

A Bantustan (in Afrikaans *Bantoestan*) was a territory the National Party set aside for Black inhabitants of South Africa and South West Africa (now Namibia). The term, first used in the late 1940s, was coined from Bantu (meaning "people" in some of the Bantu languages) and - stan - a suffix meaning "land" in the Persian language and some Persian-influenced languages of western, central, southern Asia and Eastern Europe. It became a disparaging term by some critics of the Apartheid-era government homelands. Apart from establishing ten homelands in South Africa, the government also established ten in neighbouring South West Africa, that were under South African administration at the time.

Had someone asked me to describe the students, I would have said they were curious, radical, politicised, anti-White, snobbish, non-participatory, poor and racists.

A White student asked where I was from when he heard my foreign accent and, while pointing to the colour of my skin, raised the tone of his voice for other students to hear. "You mustn't worry in this country," he told me. "You'll be okay as white is your lucky skin colour!" I perfectly understood the meaning of his words, as Whites were, in fact, enjoying a privileged status under Apartheid. I also knew that as a foreigner, nothing would be served to me on a platter just because of the colour of my skin.

Then one beautiful sunny but wintry day in 1984, whilst studying in English, a language I was just starting to comprehend, I needed to take a break. That is when my weary eyes fell upon gorgeous features partially hidden by a mystical light blue scarf. "Who's that girl? I've never seen her before." She radiated beauty, and I could not keep my eyes off her. Dare I talk to her because my first impression was that of a woman not easily approachable? She was a Muslim student with a striking light-brown complexion and a slender, shapely figure.

I had never met a Muslim before and would only later learn that they were generally conservative. I decided to approach her the straight-forward Italian way: "Hi, how're you? I'm Elio, nice to see you at the library. I never saw you here before. Are you a new student?" My words were met by silence and an expression bordering on disbelief. I do not even recall what she said immediately after, but she somehow acknowledged my greetings without getting annoyed at my direct, unconventional ways. Something told me I could not be too assertive. I smiled, and returned to my desk, already planning my next move. I had at least managed to get her name: "Asheeqah", which in Arabic means "Beloved", a name which sounded like music to my ears. Little did I know the emotional turmoil Asheeqah would cause in my young life.

Every time I saw Asheeqah in the library, it was like a mystical vision. Even though we had exchanged some intense looks, we never really engaged in a conversation until, one day, I decided to approach her again and ask about her studies. That is when she opened up and spoke freely about her interest for private and family law. Bedazzled by her, I listened but hardly heard a thing. I was just drinking in her shining beauty. "Where do you stay?" I asked. "I live in Bosmont, a 30-minute bus drive from here, on the western side of the city." Bosmont was predominantly Coloured, with many following the teachings of the Holy Quran. "I've never been to Bosmont but maybe one day I'll make a turn there!" I quickly replied.

Winning her trust months later, the time arrived for me to visit the suburb where Asheeqah lived with her family. I was to meet her not far from the local mosque, because I could not visit her home as the family, particularly her brothers and father, would never approve of our friendship. In fact, she had not mentioned our relationship to anyone. As I did not own a car, I asked her if I could pick her up on a motorbike, a Honda 200 which a friend had lent me to move around Joburg. She had never ridden on a motorbike before and was a bit hesitant when she heard about the two-wheeler. "No worries, I'll have a helmet for you. Besides, no one in your community will recognise you once you wear it!"

I was tense when I headed to my first date with Asheeqah in Bosmont. I thought there would be little hope for me to conquer her heart, because of our widely different backgrounds. She was Muslim from a strict family and I a free-spirited Roman Catholic. I was exploring and enjoying life, not ready for any commitment; she was more grounded and stable. We both had Apartheid standing in the way as a constant factor reminding us of our differences. "Why am I even trying to get into her life if this relationship is probably not going to work?" I repeatedly asked myself. But the desire to get to know her kept burning inside me; I simply could not stop thinking about the girl with the mystical scarf.

There she was, close to the mosque, waiting for me to pick her up. I slowly rode down the road keeping the revs to a minimum to avoid drawing the attention of residents living nearby. I greeted her with my usual smile and quickly passed her the helmet. "Hold on tight but don't unbalance me with sudden moves or we'll both fall off and then there'll be a lot for us to explain," I told her as she hid her face inside the helmet.

"Look! There's your family running to stop us!" I joked.

"Don't say that! I'll have serious problems if they see us together and, on top of it, on a motorbike! You'll have a boxing match with my brothers!" She laughed as we raced off.

We spent the afternoon at a local park talking about our lives, studies, desires and aspirations.

She spoke highly of her family and the way they brought her up, describing her dad as a charitable man and her mom as an exceedingly gracious woman who enjoyed reading love stories. Her brothers and sister were also devoted Muslims. She spoke of her ancestral roots; on her father's side, they could be traced back to the Indonesian island of Java and, on the mother's side, to a mix of Indian, Indonesian and Dutch blood. She hated having been classified by the Apartheid government as 'Coloured' for the purpose of racial identity. "The reality is that I'm a South African-born 'Muslimah' (woman of Muslim faith)." She shared the exploitation and slavery members of her family were subjected to: "My father told me some Asians arrived in South Africa from Indonesia and Malaysia at the end of 1600s during the Dutch colonial era. They were shipped to the Cape of Good Hope by the Dutch East India Company," she said sadly. "My people, like Black South Africans, have also experienced the evil of discrimination. They were first slaves of the Dutch; then exploited as 'indentured' or contracted labourers by the British for cheap labour on the plantations, railways and mines of the then-colonial Natal; then victimised by the Apartheid system."[10]

Asheeqah became emotional. "My family pulled through and we're a happy, united, middle-class family. We live in a nice home and my siblings and I've a good education." I could sense her pride for what her family had achieved despite the difficult circumstances.

Our friendship blossomed with many ups and downs, joys and disappointments. We met frequently at the university and even though she was not a coffee lover, I often convinced her to take short breaks and have a cappuccino across the road at the Brazilian coffee shop with me. I could see people staring at us, and assumed it was either because they despised the fact that a White guy and an Indian girl were clearly happy socialising in Apartheid times, or perhaps they were jealous. She was an attractive girl!

There was certainly a great rapport between us although deep inside of me, I knew it was too good to last. Sadly, the end came when, one day, she broke the news that she was leaving South Africa to join her "husband-to-be", who was also a devoted Muslim. "I'll be missing my country and also the time we spent together," she said in tears. "I understand, you need to follow your destiny, that's 'Maktub', meaning: 'It is written' or 'It is already known to Allah'. I knew that one day, I would have to mention this Arabic word to you." It was hard to say goodbye. That mystical vision I had the first day I saw Asheeqah at the library would not easily dissipate.

Mind those bombs and flying bullets

My sister's decision to leave South Africa, following some disagreements with her husband, brought about sudden unexpected changes to my life. I had to look for alternative accommodation and did not have a clue where to start searching from the comfort of a suburb like Norwood. At the time, I was living in a rondavel in their backyard. I spent many sleepless moonlit nights staring at the thatch roof with its exposed beams, watching massive rain spiders crawling about. There were also the super-sized, alien looking King crickets, colloquially known as Parktown Prawns, running awkwardly across the floor, hissing. One even attacked me and scratched my leg as I was trying to push it out of my room. That is when I realised there was something very different in Africa. Even the smallest creatures in the animal kingdom were not only three times the size of the creatures back home, but also much more threatening.

The opportunity to relocate came when my Greek Cypriot friend Kyriacos mentioned his brother had decided to go back to Cyprus and offered to share his flat in a modest building in Cyrildene, a middle-class suburb approximately 10 km from the city centre. My bed became a sleeper couch in the sitting room since Kyriacos was not giving up or sharing his bedroom. But it did not matter to me. I would have slept on the floor, if necessary. I was also more mobile now, since Kyriacos had inherited his brother's car, an old work horse Datsun from the '70s. Now we were able to move around Joburg, especially in the late afternoons and evenings, when we headed first to the Sam Busa gym in Hillbrow, then to Pizzeria Romana, in Pretoria Street, where we would queue for some time to enter.

One evening in the gym, a seemingly harmless comment once again, brought home the reality of Apartheid. Wrapped in a towel after a refreshing shower, one of the gay patrons, knowing I was Italian, scanned my body from head to toe, exclaiming: "Wow, you have a body like Michelangelo's David!" With my firm belief in the motto "live and let live", I laughed at his flattery, knowing this was one of the few places in which he, like many homosexuals, felt safe. Apartheid laws listed homosexuality as a crime punishable by up to seven years in prison. The conservative Afrikaner Dutch Reform Calvinists held a strong belief that homosexuality was unnatural and therefore sinful, and this became a major pillar of Apartheid. Homosexuals found enclaves where they felt safer to express themselves. Hillbrow was one such enclave. Not that it was necessarily safe. Undercover cops often prowled the gyms and clubs, looking for victims to snare then throw in jail.

Living with Kyriacos ran smoothly – except when we had to feed our always empty bellies. Even though I was from Italy, a country famous for its rich food traditions, my culinary skills were non-existent. My mother took care of that with great pride and passion. Kyriacos was also disastrous around the kitchen. One evening he decided to cook spaghetti and threw a couple of them up to the ceiling to check if they were ready. That is what I was told: "If the spaghetti stick to the ceiling, they're ready - if they fall off, they're still not cooked." I laughed.

It was no laughing matter when Kyriacos, after meeting Maria – a Greek girl, who was the love of his life – decided to move to Pretoria where she was staying with her family.

"Go well my friend, follow your heart. I'm strong now, I'll take care of myself," I told him.

Was I?

I learnt a few lessons since I landed in South Africa. It was a country with great opportunities and natural beauty, but certainly not short of internal problems and inter-racial conflict.

Many White South Africans, including those with Italian roots, lived a cocooned life in the comfort and safety of their homes, shopping malls and suburbs - wary and prejudiced towards people of other skin colours, protected by the status quo of the time for simply being White. Even some of my own family members were narrow-minded and often passed negative judgment on Black people. They bought into the prevailing stereotypical views of the time.

Keeping an open mind, I started interacting with people of different backgrounds, particularly the students at the university library. This is where I learnt about the institutionalized disparity of the educational system. Apartheid not only actively separated the different racial groups in South Africa through its segregation policies, it also created educational inequalities by introducing The Bantu Education Act of 1952, which limited the educational potential of Black people and ensured they remained in the lower, working classes of society.

Four Afrikaans speaking universities and one English speaking university admitted only Whites, while the other five, including Unisa (but not during my time as a student), had restricted admission and segregated classrooms.[11]

The inequalities were evident in the separate schooling infrastructure for different racial groups where government spending on education was considerably more for White children and teaching staff, 96% of whom had teaching certificates. Black schools, on the other hand, were underfunded, with inadequate resources, dilapidated buildings, and a lack of textbooks, with only 15% of the teachers certified. [12]

This led to one of the bloodiest days in the history of South Africa - June 16, 1976. Afrikaans, the language considered as the "language of the oppressor" was introduced as the medium of instruction in Black schools. In response to this, several thousand pupils from various schools began to protest in the streets of Soweto township and were met with fierce police brutality. An estimated 700 people were shot and killed during the unrest that spread beyond Soweto.[13] The photo of 12-year-old Hector Pieterson, one of the first students shot by the police, being carried by a fellow student with his sister by his side, became an international symbol that clearly described the brutality of Apartheid. The carnage was a key moment in the fight against Apartheid, as it sparked renewed opposition against the system both domestically and internationally.

South Africa was plagued by political instability and international sanctions, but also conflict. The African National Congress (ANC), the party of Apartheid struggle icons such as Nelson and Winnie Mandela, Oliver Tambo, Walter and Albertina Sisulu, Thabo Mbeki, Ahmed Kathrada and Helen Joseph, was outlawed in 1960 and driven underground after being declared a terrorist organisation. The ban was repealed in 1990 at the beginning of the transitional negotiation period leading to the first multiracial democratic elections in 1994.

Due to the intransigence of the White authorities, one of the last options available to the ANC was to embark in an armed struggle against the regime that had, through its powerful law enforcement and not always impartial judicial system, incarcerated many of their key leaders. At the Rivonia trial of 1963-64, named after the site, north of Joburg where they were arrested, Mandela and several of his comrades were prosecuted for acts of sabotage designed to overthrow the Apartheid system. They were sentenced to life imprisonment on Robben Island, a remote island barely visible from Cape Town. Here is where he spent 18 of the 27 years of his imprisonment, along with over 3 000 political prisoners. During the trial, Mandela famously said he was "prepared to die for his ideals of a democratic and free society, in which all persons will live together in harmony and with equal opportunities."[14]

Despite the international sanctions against South Africa, which gained momentum in the '80s, the Apartheid government had managed to circumvent many years of economic boycott by using flexible – and not always legal – schemes and networks for the uninterrupted import and export of strategic goods, weapons and necessary industrial components.[15] According to the locals, the government had effectively bypassed the oil embargo with the help of Italian immigrant, Marino Chiavelli, also nicknamed "oil baron" who brokered a clandestine deal with some Arab countries in 1980 that ensured thousands of barrels a day were shipped into the country in violation of the sanctions. Chiavelli became one of South Africa's first "billionaires" and in 1984 built the plush Summer Place in Hyde Park, Sandton, now a banqueting and conference venue.

The sanctions not only had a negative impact on the economy, but also on other spheres of life. On one of my early trips back to Italy, I booked with Suid Afrikaanse Lugdiens (SAL) / South African Airways (SAA), not knowing the flight would take longer than other airlines because SAA was barred from using other African states' airspace and was forced to fly over the western Atlantic Ocean, stopping to refuel at Ilha da Sol in Cape Verde.

Sport also suffered. From the late '50s, the international federations governing various sports also sanctioned South Africa, effectively barring the country's national teams from international competitions such as the Olympics.

All sports were affected by boycotts and sanctions. As an example, the cricketing boycott was prompted by the "D'Oliveira affair" of Basil D'Oliveira, a Coloured South African, playing for the England team in 1968 who was excluded from touring South Africa. His exclusion sparked controversy and accusations against the Apartheid government. In 1989, the International Cricket Council agreed that playing in South Africa would carry a minimum 4-year ban on international selection.

In the early '80s, military and police anti-riot units had been moving into townships such as Soweto and Alexandra, to quell frequent protests by youths armed with stones and petrol bombs. Troops patrolling the townships were using Casspirs, mine and ambush–resistant vehicles developed in South Africa that could hold a crew of two, plus 12 additional soldiers. They were originally used in the South West Africa border war fought from 1966 to 1989 – also known as the Namibian War of Independence between South Africa and the People's Liberation Army of Namibia (PLAN), the military wing of the South West Africa People's Organisation (SWAPO).

During 1984, several rioting protesters were killed in townships such as Sebokeng, Boipatong and Sharpeville, south of Joburg, that had been effectively sealed off by police and the military, conducting house-to-house searches to counter not only rioters, but also criminal elements who had found fertile ground to operate amid the chaos.

Young and old, men and women, openly defied the Apartheid security forces, usually just with stones as there were not many illegal firearms in the hands of the general Black public. Those in the crowd who showed their backs while running away, risked being shot and killed with live ammunition. There would not be any official investigation into the shootings or deaths. Because of this increasing violent conflict, the government was forced to declare a state of emergency in the country.

During the '80s, South Africa also experienced a wave of deadly and destructive terror attacks by struggle groups fighting the regime. The main armed groups were the ANC's Umkhonto We Sizwe (MK) and the Azanian People's Liberation Army (APLA). Founded in 1961, MK was responsible for many acts of terrorism against the Apartheid state, targeting transportation lines, power stations and other civil infrastructure. Deriving its name from Azania, meaning land of the Black people, APLA was also launched in 1961 by the Pan Africanist Congress (PAC) as its military wing. In 1986, APLA adopted the rallying cry "one settler, one bullet", implying Whites, viewed as settlers, were in their target. The PAC's anti-White establishment stand appeared to be more extremist than that of the ANC, as it stood for the repossession of African land from foreign invaders, and the destruction of colonial supremacy. The ANC, through its 1955 Freedom Charter, believed South Africa "belongs to all who live in it, Black and White, and that no government could justly claim authority unless it is based on the will of all the people".[16]

Both sides, outlawed by the regime in 1960 with the Unlawful Organizations Act, had become involved in the armed struggle and, during my time in the country, many acts of indiscriminate terror against civilians were committed. The early '90s, a delicate transitional period characterised by the Convention for a Democratic South Africa (CODESA) negotiations, saw an increase in APLA's sanctioned attacks. It culminated in the 1993 St James church massacre in Kenilworth, Cape Town, where 11 people were gunned down during a church service. The Apartheid government hit back at the "enemies of the state" with undercover members of the security apparatus conducting what could also be described as terror activities, with raids targeting anti-Apartheid activists and members of organisations banned by the regime. Many "committed suicide" during torturous interrogations at the infamous John Vorster Square in downtown Joburg.

Innocent bystanders also died. I happened to be close to the scenes of bomb attacks. The first explosion occurred in Pretoria in May 1983, not long after my arrival in the country. I was in the car with Robi coming back from the Capital city, when we first heard a deafening bang and within a few minutes, the sound of police and emergency service sirens coming from all directions. We realised something serious had just happened. Driving back to Joburg, we heard on the radio that a powerful bomb had detonated outside the Air Force Headquarters, killing 17 and injuring more than 200. This attack intensified the regime's fight against MK militants and led to cross-border bombing raids against MK bases in Maputo, the capital of Mozambique.

The second explosion happened as I was walking downtown in 1987. Anything that had to do with police action drew my immediate attention, so I joined a crowd next to a large retail store where several police cars were present with their flashing blue lights. The police had cordoned off the front section of the store. Seconds after a police officer began shouting at the crowd in both English and Afrikaans: "Stand back! *Staan terug!*", I heard a loud bang, followed by a terrifying whistling sound. I ducked behind a car as I heard windows shattering with glass splinters flying in all directions. The explosion was caused by a device later identified as a limpet mine, often used by MK fighters. The device had been left inside the store during peak trading time and was designed to cause injury and death. Fortunately, security personnel had spotted it in time. Shaken, I realised the country was not as stable as many people told me when I arrived. "Phew, that was a close shave! I foresee some real troubles ahead," I thought to myself, remembering Italy's *Anni di Piombo* (Years of Lead) during the '70s and early '80s when that country also experienced several terrorist attacks committed by both far-left and far-right extremist groups, albeit with different ideologies and objectives.

My prediction was right. 1987 was a year of terror in Joburg. Those like me, who regularly went to the city for work and study, were on the edge every time we happened to be next to a refuse bin in a public area. "Maybe it concealed a limpet mine?" "Maybe I'll be the victim today?" When walking or waiting for a bus, I stayed as far away as possible from any place which could be used by terrorists to hide an explosive device. In that year alone, powerful car bombings shook downtown Joburg outside the Magistrate's Court, and a military headquarter, causing multiple casualties.

It was clear that the ANC, through its military wing, had stepped up its fight against the Apartheid state. Some MK cadres received training in guerilla warfare in countries such as the Soviet Union, in what was then the German Democratic Republic and closer to home, neighbouring Mozambique and Angola, at the time both under Soviet influence. Their strategy appeared to be that of targeting buildings of symbolic importance where many bystanders could be maimed or killed. They often caused small explosions with limpet mines to lure the police to a specific area, only for these to be followed by deadly car bombs, aimed at inflicting maximum damage and casualties. Causing fear and panic among the population, especially in areas known to be under the control of Whites, was part of the objectives.

But there was another side of the coin. Some White fanatics with an extremist ideology and a mix of racial, religious and supremacist motives, were out for revenge. I clearly recall the 1988 Strijdom Square massacre in Pretoria where a smiling Barend Strydom, dubbed "*Die Wit Wolf*" or "The White Wolf", randomly took aim and, one by one, killed eight and injured 16 people. Seven of the victims were Black, while one was Indian. During his trial, he claimed his intention was to instigate a race war and that he had acted according to the will of God, for the survival of his people, the Afrikaners. He was sentenced to death by hanging, a practice the regime he claimed to defend had introduced but was released from prison in 1992 as a political prisoner by the then President FW de Klerk.

In 1994, the mass killer was granted amnesty by the Truth and Reconciliation Commission (TRC). The TRC's core mission was to uncover truths about severe human rights violations spanning from March 1960 to May 1994. Formed by Nelson

Mandela to "heal the nation", it was chaired by Archbishop Desmond Tutu, who famously coined the term "Rainbow Nation", encapsulating South Africa's racial diversity. The TRC allowed freedom fighters, Apartheid agents and families seeking closure on family members who had disappeared during the struggle, to seek amnesty and listened to about 21 000 victims in over 2 500 hearings. Operating under the Department of Justice and Constitutional Development, the TRC's recommendations are still being put into action, including compensating victims, creating appropriate memorials, offering medical support, aiding affected communities, and providing educational bursaries to descendants of Apartheid-era victims.

In 1995, the death penalty was abolished by the constitutional court.

When I arrived in the '80s, the country was in the midst of civil unrest where violence, racial protests, riots and political repression were part of the circumstances of the time. Crime was not an issue – at least not for Whites. I walked from the clubs in Hillbrow or downtown Joburg in the middle of the night and early morning hours without being stopped and harassed by anybody, not even drunks or vagrants who were invisible those days, hiding in dark alleys between high-rise buildings. The risk when visiting pubs and clubs was getting involved in brawls with local guys, sometimes over pretty girls, sometimes just for futile issues. Cars parked at night in city streets were perfectly intact the following day; police were showing their presence in their unmistakable yellow Ford Cortinas and Ford Sierras. There were no high walls with razor wires and spikes or electric fences protecting residential and business premises, and very few security systems linked to a control room and armed response. I did not hear gunshots, just sporadic distant police sirens, a normal feature of a large, bustling city. "Can this be for real? How can this place be so safe to walk around in?"

I soon discovered the reality was different. Because the Apartheid government had deployed its law enforcement agencies in the fight against political violence, crime had increased significantly across South Africa by the mid '80s. However, this phenomenon was more prevalent in townships and informal settlements, plagued by social issues such as unemployment, poverty, alcohol, drug abuse, gangsterism and over-crowding. Coupled with the availability of illegal weapons and an absence of community services, it was a recipe for crime.

The lack of regular police activities such as crime prevention and investigations created near-anarchy with criminals literally getting away with murder. Rapists easily targeted victims of all ages without fearing arrest and prosecution. Mob or vigilante justice reprisals and lynching attacks were gruesome. One brutal method was the "necklace". Innocent or not, a car tire filled with fuel was placed around the neck of the suspect and set alight - the crowd ululating as their victim died an agonising death. This method of killing became common practice in the townships in the '80s, especially against people who were suspected of collaborating with the Apartheid authorities. They were called "impimpis".

While this brutal scenario played out in Black areas, Whites lived in safe suburbs, many of them turning a deaf ear and keeping a blind eye to the atrocities inflicted against the Black population.

Finding employment and earning an income was easier for Whites as the country's economy was firmly in their hands. The notion of Black Economic Empowerment (BEE), aimed at redistributing wealth to the population who had been sidelined by Apartheid, was not part of the corporate agenda. It became part of the new government's policies addressing the injustices of the past. But then, the Apartheid state with its bureaucratic apparatus was a big employment basket for Whites – Afrikaners above all – leaving much smaller scale informal/trading economy in the townships and settlements up to the Black people.

It was not long before I could hear the whistling of the first bullets flying dangerously close to me.

As the '90s dawned, the regime moved to relax certain Apartheid laws, such as the Group Areas Act – and the floodgates of crime opened.

The relaxation of entry at the borders and the halting of control of the movement of Blacks through the so-called pass laws with the abolition of the Influx Control Act in 1986, meant thousands flocked to the cities in search of opportunities, including undocumented foreigners who crossed over to South Africa illegally.

Escaping economic and political hardships in their country of origin, initially from Zimbabwe, Mozambique and Malawi but later even from far-away countries such as Nigeria, Congo, Somalia and Ethiopia, the refugees flocked in.

This contributed to chaotic situations in the cities, particularly Joburg, as high-rise buildings and landlords in areas such as Hillbrow and surroundings experienced overcrowding, non-payment of property levies and city rates, and even hijacking of entire buildings from legitimate owners. Slowly, criminal elements infiltrated the city and its suburbs, increasing the risk for law-abiding citizens falling victim to fraudsters, robbers and rapists. This brought about a rapid decline in the standard of living and a disintegration of law and order.

Criminal elements moved freely and acted with impunity as the police began to lose morale as experienced personnel left in droves to join the better-paying and managed private security industry.

Joburg was now a dangerous place, not only for me, but also for my "Italian Stallion" friend Mario, who painted the town red with me. Mario, like many other foreigners, had decided to leave soon after the end of the White minority rule sanctioned by the first democratic elections of 1994, which saw the ANC win the majority vote. He was never able to accept and adapt to these mammoth social and political changes and no longer believed in this country's future. Being older, he felt unsafe, yes – but being wiser, he also realised business opportunities were slowly but surely fading away as companies began to implement Black Economic Empowerment policies, which saw Black entrepreneurs, some with questionable experience and integrity, winning most of the contracts he previously tendered for.

On his way to his native Verona, I had to say a difficult goodbye to my friend at the airport. Our voices were trembling as we hugged and wished each other good luck. I still today hear his wish for me as he slowly, almost reluctantly, walked down the corridor: *"Goditi la vita!"* - "Enjoy your life!".

That was still far in my future. Now, in the mid-'80s, I said goodbye to the safe suburbs and found a small, furnished apartment in Hillbrow, the ideal location for a student with little money. Many foreign expats had made Hillbrow their home; it was vibrant, clean and safe. I could, in the middle of the night, pop in at the Fontana supermarket in High Point – the highest place in Joburg, in terms of altitude – for one of their famous roasted chickens. Estoril was a great international bookshop where I could buy Italian newspapers and magazines to keep up with the latest news from my home country – and how can I forget that little corner place where a stocky German sold bratwursts on a roll? Then there was Doney restaurant where I celebrated my graduation when I obtained my first Bachelor of Arts degree? What about Mirella's and Carlo's coffee shops? They were two of my favourite spots to study over a cappuccino.

However, Hillbrow had its dark side. Many people died there. In the many dodgy looking streets and alleys, you could meet the suburb's wicked, with vices in brothels, prostitutes and zombie-like creatures devastated by lethal substances. Sure, it was a liberal place to live in - certainly more than the conservative Pretoria just 50 km away. But this freedom came with risk.

I recall the night when I went alone to a club in the heart of Hillbrow, a place I occasionally frequented with Mario. Tom, the bouncer, a muscular and tough Black guy, knew me and always treated me with respect. I knew that if some bad elements gave me trouble, I could rely on him to sort things out, so I always tipped him well. That night, I greeted him as usual. "You're welcome, please come in," he said, giving me the thumbs-up.

While listening to the DJ's unmistakable '80s disco beat, I heard a commotion and loud screams coming from the entrance of the club. Patrons were scattering in all directions. It was Tom having an argument with a much smaller guy. As I looked down the passage, I saw him pulling out a gun and fire four shots at Tom at very close range in rapid succession. I ducked for cover behind a large pillar as the shooter made a quick escape into the dark alleys. There was Tom, lying on the cold floor of the club that had employed him to keep undesirable elements at bay, gasping for air. "I'm dying - I'm dying." – and he did.

The blood was also flowing on the night I introduced "my" city to Ilario, a new friend from my hometown in Italy. As a qualified vet, he had relocated to South Africa to further his studies. After an initial period at a university close to Pretoria, specialising in veterinary studies, he moved to Joburg, lodging with an Italian family who had emigrated in the '60s. They lived in Bez Valley, a suburb in the east of Joburg. Their children were all born in South Africa, and like many Whites at the time, they lived in the comfort of their cocoon, frequenting places where they felt safe, as far away as possible from the "*swart gevaar*" or "black danger" - especially Hillbrow, where risk and vice lived side-by-side.

Ilario jumped at the chance to discover town, especially after I assured him, I knew each and every corner and alley of the city and he would be perfectly safe. It was 8pm and we were hungry, so I took him to the famous pizzeria Il Padrino (The Godfather) in downtown Joburg. Walking towards the restaurant we saw blue police lights flashing and spotted a body. "But that's a dead body!" Ilario exclaimed.

"Yes, it looks as if someone has just been shot near the place where we're heading to."

As we approached the crime scene, I heard bystanders talking about a man who had been killed by the police when he attempted to escape, following a robbery at a nearby store.

"You know, Joburg is a big city, things are happening here, but don't worry, you're with me. Let's go and have our pizza," I told a shaken Ilario who came from a small town where virtually nobody ever was killed, therefore had never seen a murdered person before.

Murder aside, the pizza was good as Tonino the *pizzaiolo* or pizza maker was one of the best in town.

When we left The Godfather, the night was still young. "Let's go have a coffee in Hillbrow," I told Ilario, describing an Italian coffee bar frequented not only by Italians but also other Europeans, Greeks and Portuguese in particular. "You'll like it there; it's a fun place where one can sit on the balcony and admire the ladies walking by."

"I hope it'll be safer there!"

"Sure, I know the place and owners well. It's really a cool spot." I replied.

The owner was a hot-headed Sicilian whose volatile temperament often landed him in hot water. There, is where I interacted with a cross section of members of the Italian community. Some were successful entrepreneurs, especially in engineering, construction and importing of goods. Others were devious characters living by their wits, gambling, playing cards and spending hours around a table, swearing and causing a great deal of commotion to the astonishment of new patrons. In general, the Italian community was well-respected by the more conservative English and Afrikaner. They were known to be skilled workers with excellent manual dexterity and good artistic flair.

At that time of the night, Hillbrow was buzzing with people.

"*Ciao ragazzi, come va stasera*?" - "Hi guys, how're you tonight?" The owner of the coffee shop welcomed us.

"*Ciao*, all good, Toni. We're here for a nice espresso."

"Sure, take it easy and relax. It's a nice evening."

Chatting over our coffees, we were abruptly interrupted by the clear sound of gun shots as people scattered in all directions.

Suddenly, there was mayhem and pandemonium very close to where we were sitting. "Dive flat under the table!" I screamed to Ilario who, without any hesitation, obeyed my order while many rounds of ammunitions were being fired in the immediate vicinity of the coffee shop.

"Stay down, stay down!" I kept on shouting. Not less than 20 shots were fired in what appeared to be a drive-by shooting between rival gangs.

When the gunfight was over, pushed by my "police instinct", I took a brief walk not even 20 metres away from where we were sitting. There, in the middle of upturned tables and chairs, were the bodies of three people riddled with bullets, shot dead as they sat enjoying their meal.

Ilario was numb: "It can't be true! This place is bloody dangerous! Where else in the world, does one experience four people getting killed in one night, in the space of three hours between a pizza and an espresso?!"

I never intended to expose him to that kind of ordeal during his first night out in the city. "He'll probably pack his suitcase and rush back to crime-free Montebelluna," I thought.

But he did not. In fact, our friendship grew stronger, and Ilario continued his life in South Africa after having learned in a single bloody night how to duck for cover to avoid flying bullets.

African heart

It was a difficult time in my life. I was feeling down and vulnerable without my family and closest friends in a country where I still could not fully adapt. I felt as if I still had one foot in Italy, not really knowing whether South Africa would be the right place for me to settle in and fulfil my career ambitions. There I was, alone and sad in the middle of a concrete jungle trying to make sense of my young life.

My visits to Mrs Sartor, whom I had met in the Brazilian Coffee Shop in what felt like a lifetime ago, became more frequent, with many lunches and suppers shared with her family. One evening, I went with them to an Italian cultural centre in Kensington where their son was a DJ. I got on well with Mrs Sartor's daughter Mara, but our relationship always remained within the boundaries of a simple and genuine friendship.

It was when I moved over to the coffee counter to get my much-loved cappuccino that my heart skipped a beat. I saw a well-dressed, good-looking Black girl, visibly battling to serve the crowd. "Wow, she's really cute!" I thought, pushing my way in to get an even better look at her. She was wearing a bright purple shirt that made her nice features stand out. Her hair was long and naturally curly.

It took a couple of orders at the counter for her to finally notice me. I immediately sensed she was afraid of interacting with me because, on the one side, there were many patrons around and, on the other, the Apartheid-instilled mindset was a big impediment to freedom of expression between people of different races.

I jotted down my name and home number on a small piece of paper and discreetly slipped it to her when she came closer.

"I can see you're too busy to talk now. Please call me when you can. I'd really like us to chat. By the way, what's your name?"

"My African name is Naledi, which means star, but Trudy is my English name," was the timid answer.

"Hope to talk to you soon, Naledi. Your first name sounds very nice to my ears!" I said, before joining the Sartor family again.

Days went by - Nothing. Then one afternoon the phone rang. Even though we had only exchanged a couple of words the night we met amid the noisy crowd, I immediately recognised her voice. "You're Naledi, the pretty lady from the cultural centre!" It was quite a mission to understand each other with our heavy accents, but just before the public telephone line cut, as she was running out of coins, we agreed to meet the coming weekend at the coffee shop of a hotel close to the airport.

Heading to the hotel I had mixed feelings, as I had never dated a Black girl before, and knew that both White and non-White South Africans frowned upon mixed couples. Besides, I had my doubts she would remember the date, since she had no phone at home, and I could not call her back to confirm the details. "Maybe she changed her mind about dating a White guy," I thought, as the clock turned 8.30pm, one hour after we had agreed to meet. "Where the hell is this girl? Should I leave or wait a bit more?" Something inside me told me to hold on a bit longer, but close to 9pm my patience ran out. While walking to the parking lot, in the distance, I saw a Black girl coming toward me with a big smile on her face.

How could I not forgive her tardiness, I thought, looking at her innocent face. Naledi was accompanied by a female friend who stayed timidly in the background, so it was not quite the private date that I had in mind.

"I'm very sorry for being late," Naledi said softly. "It's not easy for us to travel as we've no car. We had to catch a train from Tembisa, a township in the East Rand, and walk from the station to a taxi rank and from the street where they dropped us off, we had to walk again to meet you here".

"I also decided to come with my best friend, as I was a bit nervous to travel on my own at night. You know, it's dangerous for us ladies to be alone in the streets at night. In fact, on the way here, we were followed and harassed by some bad guys but, luckily, we arrived safe!"

Of course, I had forgotten about the hardship of travel for Black people. My fellow students often told me of the daily sacrifice it required to reach the Unisa library - standing in long queues waiting for a train or taxi – and not the European vision of the taxi as a fancy car. No, taxis used by Black people were, and still are minivans capable of cramming more passengers than legally allowed and are often in a poor state of roadworthiness. They are a real danger to both commuters and road users. But it was a cheap way to get around.

Frankly, I did not know where to go to with the two ladies that night; it was our first date and I needed to know if there could be others, before venturing out to restaurants or clubs, knowing the dangerous beast out there named Apartheid. "Let's go to my flat, I'll prepare a nice plate of pasta with my favourite sauce. You must be hungry!" I knew my culinary skills were bad, but here was I offering dinner.

There, in the safety of my flat, Naledi and her friend could talk freely, telling me about their life, families and dreams. Listening to their stories, I realised that no matter the colour of your skin, we all have feelings, emotions, aspirations, and intelligent minds. We all want to live a decent life. We all wish to be treated with fairness and respect. But the sad reality is that some of us, from the time we are born, grow up in disadvantaged families and environments, trapped by a vicious cycle of poverty that deprives one of opportunities – and sometimes, even the most basic things in life.

That evening was the beginning of a very long journey with Naledi, as my African heart slowly began to beat faster and faster.

I just had to see with my own eyes how Black people lived in their forcibly designated "locations" or "kasi", a short version of *lokasie*, the Afrikaans word used to describe the townships. I was always warned against going to the "wolf's den", until a fellow student invited me to Tembisa. He knew where Naledi lived, and I jumped at the chance.

Passing some neatly organised White suburbs, my "township guide" entered an area with dusty roads and hundreds of cheap, poorly constructed little homes, almost all shaped the same, some with unfinished and unpainted walls. With infrastructure sorely lacking in all townships, there were no streetlights – only spotlights on high poles lighting up blocks at a time – and no sewerage system. The pit toilets in most backyards were basically a deep hole in a concrete slab, where the user "squatted and dropped", covered by a structure also known as an outhouse. These toilets functioned without water.

"How privileged are those who live in well-developed suburbs, blessed with solid, comfortable homes with all the necessities?" I thought.

"There's Naledi's home; the one painted in yellow with the number 497 on the front wall. Let's see who's there!"

We knocked at a peeling, discoloured steel door. I will never forget her mother's wide eyes when she saw me standing there. Naledi had told her about me, but we had not met in person.

"I'm Elio, I'm here to pay my respects to you and your family."

"I'm Linah, Naledi's mom," she answered in English "You're welcome, please come in."

The room was furnished with essentials: a small couch in the right corner where I sat, and a tiny coffee table with one chair at the centre.

It was a cold day, and I wondered how they heated their home with no access to electricity; a strong smell in the house told me the family was using a coal stove to cook and keep warm, just like my grandma did to warm her cold country house during the harsh Italian winter.

There was no TV set, like in most White homes, only a tiny radio blaring out local gospel music. The floor was a cold concrete slab with no carpet. A simple curtain separated the sitting room from the sleeping areas.

I suddenly saw the curtain moving. It was Naledi, who had heard my voice but did not expect me as I could not reach her in time to inform her of my impending visit. The only way I could talk to her was by calling her neighbours, who were fortunate enough to have a telephone. If their son, Butinyana, answered, he would look for Naledi and tell her I was on the other side of the line – but if the father reached the phone first, he would slam it down on me. "Damn it, can't you be a little more sympathetic?" But I also understood he did not want to be bothered by any White man.

Her face lit up when she saw me: "What a surprise! Now you can see with your own eyes where I live!" I was served a cup of tea while Naledi entertained me with tales of her youth. "I grew up in a village in Northern Transvaal, now known as Limpopo, near Tzaneen, a farming area. Mom and dad had to come to Joburg looking for jobs.

We come from an area known as Modjadji, named after the first Rain Queen, where the Balubedu people lived happily and in harmony.

Let me tell you something about my place that I think you'll like. Our local queen is believed to have magic powers; she can control the clouds and rainfall. It may sound strange to you, and you probably won't believe it, but that's why our village is blessed with fertile soil and good vegetation!"

Naledi's passion and pride in her people was evident, but the hardship also showed.

"My granny looked after my sisters, my brother and I while our parents were away. My dad works as an assistant truck driver for a logistics company, and my mom is a domestic worker for an Afrikaans-speaking family."

Her mom was watching my reactions carefully. "Ah, now I know why you're fluent in Afrikaans," I told her – and I could see the acceptance in her eyes.

After spending eye-opening hours with them, heading back to the city I kept on seeing the dusty roads and tiny house – but I knew that Naledi's family might have been materially poor, but was rich in soul.

Freedom to choose, freedom to love – at a price

Being with Naledi was not easy. It was against the Apartheid laws, which prohibited love across the colour line.

"Can it really be a crime for me to share my feelings with Naledi? Can it be possible for the Apartheid state to interfere in the private lives of its citizens to such an extent that they are forced apart? This has got to be sheer madness! I can't accept it. I'm a free man from a free country, free to be with whoever I want and free to love whoever I choose to!"

As a mixed couple we had to fight an unjust system and overcome a judgmental public with entrenched societal stereotypes of inferior Blacks and superior Whites.

"How can he go out with a Black girl, isn't he ashamed?" This was probably the question in many people's mind when they saw me with Naledi.

I had an answer for them: "Why can't these people understand that human feelings are universal? That we're all equipped with sentiments of love and care for others? Can't they see and appreciate the inner potential of everyone when we're given a chance to have equal opportunities, education and respect for human rights and dignity?"

But that was not all. Being with Naledi was also a logistical nightmare. Many restaurants in White areas barred Black people. "Where can I go with Naledi and be left in peace to enjoy her company?" This was the question I always had to ask, to avoid racist elements ready to provoke a fight.

"To hell with that! She must be able to come wherever I go!" I told myself. In reality, I carefully avoided venues where she could be humiliated. This was one of my main concerns. To avoid Naledi encountering situations where she could be belittled by arrogant, ignorant people because, above all else, I cared about her dignity.

Other problems popped up too. When we walked the streets of Hillbrow or downtown Joburg, or drove in my car, we had to endure racist remarks shouted at us from passing police vehicles. One night we came across a police patrol unit and heard one of the cops venting his rage at us in Afrikaans.

And how can I forget the humiliations Naledi had to face when her own people – taxi drivers in particular – hurled abuse at her for being with a White man. *"Uyisifebe!"* - "You're a whore!" was one of the first swear words I got to know in a local native language.

Because of my classical school background, this human and cultural decline reminded me of the European period between the 5th and 14th centuries known as the "Dark Ages" – but there were also glimpses of hope. I will never forget when during a cold winter's day in Joburg, Naledi and I decided to have lunch at a restaurant in High Point where we could warm ourselves, away from the freezing winds racing between Hillbrow's skyscrapers. We had been there before without hassles so naturally, it became a place where we felt comfortable. This is where we spent some of the little money we had for "special occasions". The treat we could afford was hake or calamari with rice or chips, with ketch-up and tartar sauce brought to the table by a young White waitress who clearly did not mind serving mixed couples. It was not a typical Italian dish, but it was tasty enough when hunger struck.

We were sitting in a quiet corner with two White Afrikaans couples enjoying their food at a table not far from ours. Out of the corner of my eye, I could see them looking at us as we spoke about our life. "You see those people? I see trouble coming," I warned Naledi.

As the group was leaving one of the men came towards us. "Oh, here comes the trouble!" I thought. The man stopped next to our table and spoke words I will never forget: "When I see the two of you sitting together, speaking freely to each other, I still have hope for the future of this country and its people!"

I recall the day I invited Naledi to the Brazilian coffee shop in downtown Joburg for a coffee break. "Let's get on the bus I often take to go to town!" I told her, forgetting it was a "Whites Only" bus. We stood at the bus stop being scrutinised by the all-White crowd. The bus arrived, punctually as usual. I cannot deny that the Afrikaners who, for the most part, occupied local and central government positions – including those of bus drivers – knew how to run public services efficiently. The doors of the bus slammed open. The first passengers jumped in. But Naledi and I were stopped. "You can come, but she's not allowed in!" The driver warned with a heavy Afrikaans accent, stretching his arm forward with his hand clearly indicating "stop". He was young, barely 30. For a moment, I thought I could reason with him. "Come on, man, please allow her to enter, we need to go downtown." I should have listened to what some Italian immigrants told me about Afrikaners. "They're stubborn, if they say no, trying to negotiate with them is hopeless."

"No! She's not allowed!" was the driver's final answer. But I could not keep quiet. "What's wrong with her? She's a human being like you and me!" He was about to throw me off the bus, whilst some passengers encouraged him to do so, and others shouted at him to allow Naledi on the bus. He slammed the door in our faces. I remember the last words I shouted to him; "Your nonsense is going to come to an end soon!"

Change was inevitable and not far from the horizon, but clearly not in this bus driver's mind. He most likely grew up in a conservative environment, possibly raised by a racist family who taught him to take discrimination as his birth right, as something legislated and enforced by the state. He behaved exactly the way the law had empowered him to act.

I tried to comfort Naledi. This was just one of many humiliations she had to suffer; she was told she could not use a public bus service, asked for a pass to justify her presence in a White area, harassed by the police who should be there to protect and serve the public with fairness and justice.

***

One day, I decided to look for new accommodation as there had been a couple of break-ins in my building. Obviously, the rent had to tick the right box as, being a student, I could only afford a place on the cheap side of town. But there was another issue, I had to move because management banned Black people from entering the building – unless they were cleaners. "How am I going to get Naledi to visit me without her being harassed for the colour of her skin?" I had heard incredible stories about multi-racial couples having to go to extremes to protect their relationships, and endure the most unjust, unfair and cruel treatment at the hands of the Apartheid police.

Friends spoke of an Eastern European man who, out of fear of being reported to the authorities for having a Black girlfriend, resorted to smuggling her inside the apartment block where he was staying in a large laundry bag. Then there was a German who, while in bed with his Black girlfriend, had a rude awakening when the police stormed his flat and took him and her half-naked to the local police station to be charged for a "crime" committed under the Immorality Act. It was clear the couple had been betrayed by racist neighbours who had informed the police. There was no crueller way to humiliate people who were only guilty of loving each other.

"There's no way I'm going to be subjected to this nonsense! I'm going to find the right place where no one will harass Naledi and I for being a couple."

I remembered there was a neat, secure building I liked, in a buzzy part of Hillbrow. I pressed the caretaker's intercom button. A man answered in Afrikaans: "*More, wat soek jy?*" - "Morning, what are you looking for?" I started explaining why I was there when, after hearing my accent, he interrupted me abruptly and in heavy Afrikaans-accented English, asked: "Are you a White European?" Did I hear correctly? "White European?"

I lost it. "Yes, I'm more European than what you think you are! You're born in Africa, and I was born in Europe!" I left, hearing him shouting: *"Gaan hel toe!* - "Go to hell!"

Off I went to my second unfortunate experience; this time at a well-looked after building not far from the first one. I was met by the caretaker, a Coloured lady in her 40s. "How can I help you?" she asked.

"I'm looking for a small flat to rent."

"You're at the right place! We've some nice units available, and you should know that this is really a good place to live as there are no *kaffirs* in this building!"

"What did she just say?" I was speechless. She had just referred to Black people in the most abusive and derogatory way by calling them "kaffir", a word with etymological roots in the Arabic word *Kafir* ("non-believer"), which nowadays amounts to extremely offensive and illegal hate speech. How could I possibly rent a flat here?

"No worries, it's not the right place for my Black girlfriend and I," I told her, leaving her speechless.

That made me realise Black people were discriminated against by Whites and Coloureds, who, after the implementation of the Apartheid laws, were also disenfranchised and forced to relocate to townships or shanty parts of town, away from White areas.

Maybe that caretaker shared the same sentiments as some of my fellow Coloured students. Many felt more in tune with their White counterparts than with Black people. I also sensed there was a feeling of betrayal amongst the members of this community. The Coloured population is inextricably intertwined with the arrival of the first Dutch settlers, accompanied by a small group of Germans, in the Cape of Good Hope, also known as Cape Town, under Jan van Riebeeck's Dutch East India company in the mid-1600s. The Dutch were followed by French Huguenots who had escaped religious persecutions in Europe and, in the early 1800s, by the first British settlers. Some of these pioneers had sexual relationships with local native women, mostly from the nomadic and pastoral Khoisan and Xhosa tribes, who worked as servants for the settlers.

However, the Coloured population was not only the result of interracial sexual relationships between White settlers and natives. Other nationalities were also forcefully brought to South Africa mainly as slaves. Some came from African countries such as Angola, Mozambique and Madagascar, others from Malaysia and India.

The mixing of races continued, assisted by Whites moving inland in search of new land to farm, away from the developing communities of the Cape colony. Initially, they moved in an eastwardly direction, along the coastline, where they encountered the Xhosa- and Zulu-speaking tribes with whom they had bloody clashes in the mid-1800s.

One such famous battle was fought on 16 December 1838, on the banks of the KwaZulu-Natal's Ncome River, now known as "Blood River", after the blood that was spilled in it. A mere 464 *Voortrekkers* ("pioneers or pathfinders"), led by Andries Pretorius, faced an estimated 25 000 to 30 000 Zulu impis or "soldiers". The death toll amounted to over 3 000 Zulu soldiers killed. Only three Voortrekker commandos were lightly wounded, including Pretorius. The Voortrekkers' battle strategy was simple. They drew their wagons into a *laager* or defensive circle with the Boers shooting from behind the safety of the wagons. The children and women reloaded the rifles with gun powder that could only shoot one shot at a time. The Zulu impis used spears, which proved no match for gun powder-operated weapons.

Other bloody battles followed with local Basotho tribes and, further north, with the Matabele and Ndebele tribes in the Voortrekkers' search for land. This search was known as the *Groot Trek* or "Great

Trek", which led to the founding of autonomous Boer republics.[17]

The primitive environment which they had to adapt to when they first arrived, the vast cultural differences and hostilities experienced when coming into contact with local tribes, their quest for self-determination with a perilous trek inland, the war with the British and the hardship of the concentration camps, are all factors that have contributed to making the Afrikaners the tough nation they have been known to be. The "closed mindedness" of some Afrikaners is described as having a "laager" mentality.

**

While searching for multi-racial accommodation, my Italian father's saying popped into my head: "*La speranza è l'ultima a morire*" or "Hope dies last". My hope came in the form of a Jewish manager of a building in a nice part of Hillbrow. The flat was small and furnished with bare essentials, but I rejoiced at his words: "Everyone is welcome here, no matter the colour of the skin, as long as they know how to behave, and we don't experience any issues or complaints from the residents."

Jump out! The Blacks are coming!

Not only buildings, but also amenities such as parks, beaches, sport centres and swimming pools in private and public areas were reserved for Whites and denied Black people access. Segregation was everywhere. There were a couple of places not far from Joburg where the Apartheid laws had less influence. One was Swaziland, an independent country, ruled by a monarchy, and the other was Bophuthatswana, the second Bantustan to be declared independent homeland by the Apartheid government in 1977.

Bophuthatswana was known for one thing among South Africans: Sun City, a resort developed by the hotel magnate Sol Kerzner as part of his Sun International group, after he struck a deal with then President Lucas Mangope. It was officially opened on 7 December 1979 and had all the forbidden fruits South Africans lusted for; gambling, topless revue shows and porn movies, all of which were banned in South Africa.

A mere 2.5 hours from Joburg, it had hotels, restaurants, swimming pools, a world-class golf course, and theatres where international stars, prohibited from performing in South Africa due to the cultural boycott, could perform. It was luxurious, surrounded by the typical African bush, close to Pilanesberg, with a game reserve where one could encounter the Big Five: lion, leopard, rhino, elephant, and the African buffalo.

"I'm going to take you to Sun City for your birthday; we'll drive and stay there for the night at the Cabanas," I told an excited Naledi. I had just bought an Audi 80 at a bargain price – R1 500 voetstoots – from a Greek leaving the country. I jumped at it, tired of buses and begging for lifts. The car was green, my favourite colour, but very old – a sort of *skorokoro* as the local Black people describe a vehicle ready to be dumped. Except for the day the engine almost caught fire, the car took me from A to B without major problems and without spending too much on fuel. In fact, while driving around town, I appreciated how cheap fuel was at the time at approximately 50c a litre.

When we checked in at the Cabanas, there was no issue at the hotel reception or with management. However, in the restaurant, I could see many curious eyes following us, with some clearly showing signs of disapproval. I had become accustomed to mean looks while walking with Naledi, so it did not really bother me. Things changed when we decided to use the swimming pool.

It was really a hot, scorching day in Sun City. One that invited guests to use the refreshing, blue pool. Naledi was the only person of colour amid a large group of Whites, mostly locals enjoying the pool, drinking litres of beer and of course, brandy and Coke – or *Klippies en Coke*, as it was called, named after a brand of brandy and a popular mixer.

We jumped in the pool and one by one, people jumped out as if Naledi had suddenly contaminated the water.

Even in the independent Black homeland of Bophuthatswana, racist attitudes were prevalent. "Damn it! These people will never change! We too are hotel guests. We've paid good money just like you and are as entitled to have fun and enjoy the facilities," I fumed.

I will never forget the look on Naledi's face. It changed from pure joy to confusion, then anger. "I know they think I'm different and that I shouldn't be here," she said, venting her frustration.

"Enjoy yourself! You're with me and we're not jumping out of this pool anytime soon! They can go back to their drinks!"

We left the next day with mixed feelings. Yes, we had fun, but the hostile reception from guests made me realise we had many challenges still lying ahead in our relationship.

As we drove back to the City of Gold, night began to fall. Gone were those gorgeous red and yellow clouds on the far horizon. We were travelling on long, straight roads surrounded by African bushveld and immersed in complete darkness, interrupted occasionally by the flickering flames of candles and lamps from the villages as we sped past.

How I love Africa!

To please my elderly parents and ensure our bond remained strong, I had planned to reunite with them at least once a year during Christmas and New Year, a magical time in Italy with snowfall, heavily laden tables with food and Christmas presents - a far cry from South Africa's summer holidays. I had not been home for almost three years, so during one of our not-so-frequent calls due to costs, I told them; "I just purchased a ticket to fly back home! I'll see you soon, promise."

With my help, Naledi found a job at Sant'Anna, a classy Italian restaurant in Sandton, a short 20-minute drive from Hillbrow.

"While I'm away, you can live at my flat in Hillbrow. It's better. Tembisa is too far." I told her.

She jumped at the opportunity. "Thank you, and although it isn't safe for a single woman in Hillbrow these days, I'll fend for myself while you are in Italy."

I admit I was worried about her safety too. She would have to spend long hours at the restaurant, including late nights, and we both knew criminal elements had creeped into Hillbrow.

The day came when I had to kiss Naledi goodbye at the airport. "I've a present for you, Elio," she said and handed me a book on Shaka Zulu, the fierce warrior King of the Zulu's and founder of the Zulu empire in Southern Africa between 1816-1828. "I wrote a message for you on the first page – a wish for you to come back soon. I'll be missing you!"

"Keep safe and stay strong, if you need me, I'll be there for you," were my last words to her.

***

It was good to be home to feel the warmth and love of my family and the strong, genuine bond I shared with my friends. But something inside me was changing. The captivating spirit of Africa, the independence and love I had experienced there, were like a magnet. My mind kept wandering back to open spaces, sunshine, crystal-clear skies and intense moments and challenges of living in a new world. I was being drawn back to the Rainbow Nation who helped me become a sensible and better person. Nothing was ever going to be the same again.

Whenever I opened Naledi's book, I felt a crushing sensation in my chest and heart. It definitely did not help my nostalgia when I realised the television series Shaka Zulu was being broadcast on Italian television.

I was restless.

The "call of Africa" reached its peak, when I had an amazing dream. It started with a sense of nightmarish fear, but ended with a feeling of joy, tranquillity and well-being. The dream was so vivid and powerful that I can still remember it.

I was in a plane when suddenly, the plane began to shake violently. Panic ensued amongst all the passengers, but I strangely remained calm thinking how to stay alive. Just then I spotted a parachute, quickly grabbed it and strapped it on me, as the plane began to disintegrate. I saw an open gap next to me and launched myself into the unknown. I felt a sense of relief when I realised the parachute had opened, slowing my fall. With the icy wind blowing fast and furious in total darkness, the scary thought of falling into the open sea almost paralysed me.

Suddenly, the strong wind stopped, and a sense of calmness took over. The darkness of the night began to dissipate as the faint lights of a small village appeared below me. I could see tiny boats floating in water. It was a fishing village. I saw a group of villagers curiously looking up at me. And I noticed their black skins. "They're African people!" I thought in wonder. As I fell onto the hard African soil, I was immediately surrounded by a group of young women who told me not to be fearful and to follow them to their huts where they would take care of me. I was back in Africa after an incredible journey.

The dream was so real, telling me the spirit of Africa had entrenched itself inside of me and would never let go.

One evening, the phone rang. "There's a girl speaking in English, asking for you," my mother said. I had not told my family the depth of my relationship with Naledi. My parents and sister in particular, knew of her but had shown clear signs of disapproval. Not only was she a foreigner, she was also Black and therefore almost an alien to them. "Will I ever get them to accept this relationship?" I thought.

I knew it could only be Naledi calling – but why? I picked up the phone with a sense of dread. "Hi Naledi, how're you? Is there a problem?"

Crying desperately, she tried to explain what had happened to her. "I've been attacked on the way back home from the restaurant, near your flat. A man put a knife to my side and asked me to follow him. He had bloodshot eyes, as if he were under the influence of drugs. He threatened to kill me if I resisted!"

She was confused and stammering, while I was trying in vain to calm her.

"He was mean, really mean. I managed to run away, banged on the door of the closest ground-floor flat, but the people refused to open. He caught up with me and again threatened me with his knife.

If he had forced me to his place, I could have been raped and killed!" she sobbed, gasping for air.

She pretended to have a child alone at home waiting for her. This, together with one of his friends calling him, is how he was distracted, and he let Naledi go. She ran to the flat, locked the door behind her and sat with her back against the door, fearing he might chase after her again and try to force his way in.

She kept on crying as she described her ordeal, explaining she had not called the police out of fear that she may be recognised when walking the same route and victimised again.

"It's just too dangerous to live here!" she cried.

"As soon as I'm back, we'll make a plan to move to a safer area," I told her after realising that the situation in Hillbrow had precipitated to a point of no return. Hers was a desperate call for help I could not ignore.

The beast is closer than you think...

Naledi did not only suffer discrimination at the hands of a ruthless government and rigid conservative societal norms. I witnessed the humiliation she had to endure from people who were brought up with racist beliefs and simply refused to accept that individuals of other races and skin colour were human beings with dignity, emotions and feelings. "How do I get them to appreciate that, despite the different socio-cultural environments, there are many good, bright people of colour who deserve to be known, heard, and treated with respect?" This question often crossed my mind.

These were also among people I knew well. People who were close to me. They were friends and family. Take the Sartor family for example, a typical close-knit Italian family. The father was a skilled artisan who could work wood in a way only Italian craftsmen could. The younger daughter Mara was a kind and gentle soul, although subjected to the mother's will. The son Marco was a dynamic guy who enjoyed his part-time work as a talented DJ playing music in clubs in downtown Joburg.

He invited me to one of the clubs where he played music. That night he also arranged a strongman competition on the dance floor where guys volunteered to hold a heavy object with straight arms for as long as possible. Thanks to my judo fitness, stamina and posture, I ended up being the second strongest man, beaten by a muscular "Boer" – but only by a couple of seconds!

The Sartors were spontaneous and generous, with solid principles rooted in their Roman Catholic faith. As immigrants, they were living a good life in South Africa. However, they always talked about their fear of Nelson Mandela being released from prison and were convinced that the country would face a revolution by the unbanned ANC. They were determined to leave South Africa if that happened.

Then they met Naledi. They were not happy about our relationship. They pretended to accept her, but eventually their true feelings were exposed.

One day, the parents ordered Mara not to go out with Naledi who was guilty of somehow having a "different" morality.

How can I forget the day when I was reproached by them for having a relationship with a Black girl.

"It can't work, you know. These people think and behave differently from us. You're going to be disappointed, and so will she. You must let her go."

"You know very well that I've true feelings for her and can't do what you're asking me to do. I'm following my heart."

At that point, I knew my relationship with the Sartors would no longer be the same. They slammed the friendship door – and I went my own way.

Their daughter was not a racist. In fact, she belonged to a generation who I was certain, would one day accept and adapt quickly to a new, non-racial South Africa. The family did leave at the time of Mandela's release from prison. So did she leave South Africa, a country she loved, to go back to Italy.

The real disappointment though came from my family – not from my father, who had briefly seen Naledi when my parents paid a short visit to South Africa. He was a kind, intelligent and understanding person. I still remember his smile as he curiously looked at Naledi with his shining blue eyes. Even though he never asked me questions about her, deep in my heart, I knew he had accepted her. Sadly, he died after a short illness. My mother and sister, on the other hand, really struggled to come to terms with the reality that Naledi had become an important person in my life.

"Why don't you find an Italian girlfriend or at least a White girl?" my mother often asked.

"Mamma, she's a good person. She cares for me and looks after me. Aren't you happy? Can't you accept it?" I repeated.

From the very beginning, my sister was very critical of my relationship. In her mind, I was being exploited by Naledi for her own benefit and that of her children. Yes, children, because Naledi had become a mom at an early age while growing up in her home village. I knew that, and I accepted it. How could I blame her for having children as a teenager outside marriage? It is a fact of life. She loved her kids. I helped with their needs when I could, despite being a rather unconventional and reserved stepfather.

I was also young with many personal issues but saw them grow up to become responsible adults. They have always respected me, even though I must have been, at least initially, a rather strange figure with very unusual habits.

I soon realised they were tormented by the fear that their mother could, one day, "run-away" to some far-away place with the man who had suddenly become the object of her affection. I also knew Naledi could rely on the ongoing support of a close and good-hearted family structure, with a mom and granny worthy of a monument – just like my granny and aunts back in Italy, who went out of their way to help my mother.

My sister opposed our relationship openly when she came to visit me in South Africa, which made Naledi feel uncomfortable and unwelcome. She was convinced Naledi was after my money. "If that was the case, Naledi wouldn't stay with me. She would find someone with real money," I told her during a heated argument. "We've a simple life, and I've very limited financial means. She's never asked me for money or complained that she had no money."

My family's negative attitude and opposition to our relationship caused a rift that isolated me from them. "How could they think that the love I've for this girl is wrong!" A rebellion started brewing inside me, keeping me from visiting them for years. "If that's the way you think, you'll force me to go my own way – whether you like it or not."

Apartheid the beast, with its inherent discrimination and prejudice, is much closer than one thinks. It is rooted deeply in some people's minds. People we know and interact with daily, people we care for, including family members. It can form part of a person's upbringing, family and cultural background. Fed by ignorance, indifference and an unwillingness to accept what they perceive as different and unworthy.

Today, people socialise with whoever they feel comfortable with. Individuals who share the same language, traditions and culture. We like people who are like us, and we are somehow reticent with those who are visibly different in the way they speak, look, think and act. I have also found it easier to engage with my countrymen whom I perceived to be "similar to me" in terms of mentality and approach to life.

The difference between the European and African way of life is striking in South Africa, with its rich cultural ethnicities and tribal traditions. However, by the time I arrived in South Africa, the Black population had already changed significantly due to increased urbanisation and exposure to Western ways – much in contrast with their traditional way of life.

What you do is wrong!

The day came when I was presented with the opportunity to join an agency involved in crime prevention and reaction. In the northern suburbs, crime was a primary concern. I met one of the senior members of the company through some friends. He happened to be of Italian descent and invited me to apply for the job.

"Why don't you join us? We need people like you with good skills and knowledge of foreign languages as we look after a large multi-lingual expat community. You'll need to wear a uniform and work a long 12-hour shift, but it's going to be fun," he said.

The starting pay was modest, but I wanted to be financially independent from my family and was eager to hold my first job in South Africa. This would allow me to have a first-hand experience of crime and security in a complex city like Joburg.

After the initial training which involved theoretical and practical sessions including target shooting, which I was really good at – I put on the full gear of the company. Dark brown trousers and a light brown shirt with red epaulettes on the shoulder, shiny black rubber shoes and of course, a 38 special in the holster, ready for the parade before the start of the first night shift.

"A bit of military-like discipline won't do any harm," I thought, as I was introduced to the armed reaction team, ready to take on the streets of Joburg. For the most part, the team were White Afrikaners, but there were also a couple of Black guys who were really good at their job.

"Welkom meneer, dit is goed om jou aan boord te hê." This translated into: "Welcome sir, it's good to have you on board." That is how I began to learn some basic Afrikaans. *"Beheer, kom in….Stuur jou boodskap…Ek is op pad,"* - "Control, come in…Send your message…I'm on the way," were typical phrases I heard on the radio network linking the control room to the response vehicles.

Very soon the "fun" the Italian manager had promised me became real, and I found myself responding to emergencies from wealthy households, chasing criminals by car and pursuing them on foot.

There was a time when, in the middle of the night, I dragged out and arrested a robber who had found a storm drain as his hide-out. I also arrested a thief who had broken into a school and hid himself by lying inside a long, flat cupboard behind a curtain. How can I forget the incredible car chase and shootout the day my colleague and I pursued a group of dangerous criminals and in the process, wrecked our response vehicle by seizing its engine.

Fun? What "fun"? We were exposed to very real danger every day. "I hope I'm not going to be sent back to my family in a body bag!" I often thought while looking up at the starry Joburg night skies. Those amazing stars were my best companions during the never-ending, tough nightshifts. Once I was wishing for a better and healthy life for me and those close to me when, suddenly, a shooting star illuminated the sky.

The "fun" also had an ugly side. Some of the officers working with me were racist towards people of colour. During a night shift, one of them vented against a Black man who had done nothing. He just happened to cross our path when the team gathered for a short break. "*Wat soek jy in hierdie buurt?*" "What are you looking for in this neighbourhood?" Because the man kept quiet, the officer interpreted it as a sign of disrespect. Encouraged by other members of the team, he began to furiously beat him up with fists and kicks without any justification. I could not sit back and witness the brutality of this attack on an innocent man. "What are you doing? This is wrong, please stop it!"

I could not let it end there. I felt obliged to report the incident to my Italian contact as a senior member of management – but the officer involved in that racially motivated incident received only a slap on the wrist and continued being part of the team. Needless to say, from that day on, we were sworn enemies. I was undoubtedly, a "traitor to the White race".

It seems that Apartheid empowered those who had the power of the law on their side. Some got away with murder with the tacit complicity of law enforcement agencies.

***

I recall the murderous spree of an unrepentant former police officer, Louis van Schoor, who later became a private security officer. During his "security duties", between 1986 and 1989, this mass murderer in uniform, mercilessly gunned down 39 people, all Blacks and Coloureds – including children – who were mostly involved in house breakings and theft. Protected by the laws of the time, which allowed police and civilians to act as if they were in the Wild West, this killer did not hesitate to shoot anyone in the back who was running away from him. While many of the killings were ruled "justifiable homicides", it took up to 1992 – a time when Apartheid was losing its strong grip – for him to be sentenced with 20 years in jail.

However, he served only 12 years before his release. In the end, almost as a "karma", a punishment for his brutal actions, he had both his legs amputated because of a serious heart condition. He is now resting, but not in peace.

Crime also followed Naledi and I...

After her attack while I was in Italy, one of the first things on my "to-do list" was to move to a safer suburb. But where? "Why don't we move to Yeoville? It's easily accessible and not too expensive," I suggested. Yeoville was known as a safe, cosmopolitan area that attracted artists, musicians, students and political activists. A large, middle-class Jewish community had been living there for many years, particularly during the '70s, frequenting the local synagogues and managing many small businesses.

During the '80s, Yeoville's social profile changed with the opening of restaurants, jazz bars, art and craft outlets, music stores and, of course, nightclubs along Rockey Street. People of all races mingled in defiance of the prevailing Apartheid laws.

So, we moved into a one-bedroom apartment in Yeoville. "It's a good move, we'll be safer here," we both thought.

We loved the vibe: from the Slow Coach café located along the main road to Mamma's pizzeria and the funky bars. Naledi finally found stable employment at an international hotel, and I was cultivating my passion for crime prevention.

However, our happiness ended abruptly. First, Naledi got accosted by a group of criminals who were after her personal belongings as she walked to the flat after work.

"They followed me, shouting at me to stop and I ran for my life. I entered a store, asked their security for help, and they walked away. I was so scared to leave the store thinking they might still be in the area waiting for me," she told me in a state of agitation.

"Damn it! We moved to this suburb thinking we'll be safer, and now we must endure this situation again!" I thought, trying to calm her down.

The second crime hit us both – close to home.

Coming back after an evening out, we found visible signs of forced entry at the house door. I entered slowly, thinking the intruders were still inside. They were gone – with some of our personal belongings. We could not believe the mess they had left.

We felt vulnerable and violated – and realised that the sense of safety we had shared up to that point was over. We looked at each other, knowing the time had come to make a drastic decision. We had to give notice immediately and make plans to move to Killarney, a nice suburb in the north of Joburg, embellished by the presence of many jacaranda trees.

"But how long is it going to last? Will the long tentacles of crime also reach that area?" I felt as if we were fugitives, running away not from the

Apartheid cops, but from the criminal elements who had given us more than one warning to get out of the areas they had slowly, but surely, taken over.

The rot also hit the Central Business District (CBD) of Joburg that I so loved.

The care-free days of the '80s when it was fun to study at the university's library and sip on my cappuccinos at the Brazilian Coffee Shop at the Carlton Centre were over forever. The elegant Koffiehuis café, the prestigious 50-storey office block, shopping centre and luxury 600 room hotel in the heart of the city where I often met Naledi, had to close because of crime and unrelenting decay. Most of the top corporate offices moved to safer areas in the northern suburbs.

By the mid '90s, the CBD became a no-go zone and a virtual ghost town. The city that was built through the sweat and sacrifices of many people both Black and White, during the frantic search for gold, was overwhelmed by signs of decay, crime and violence.

Some buildings, abandoned by their owners due to a lack of income to pay for the city rates and utilities, were taken over by gangs who, for a fee, let rooms out to squatters in a mafia-style rental racket. Filth and rubbish accumulated at street corners and many high-rise buildings were showing visible signs of neglect. Broken windows patched with plastic sheeting and rubbish bags dumped by illegal residents in alleys, forming huge stinking dumps, were visible everywhere.

The city once had well-established and efficient management structures in both local and central municipalities. With the newly formed political structures came power – and that invariably led to personal greed, risk of corruption and the inadequate preparation of a new managerial class, which was ill-equipped to take over and run the existing structures efficiently and effectively. It caused havoc with municipal services, especially in the city centre, the peri-urban and rural areas. Previously neglected and under-serviced Black townships were now also part of the municipality's responsibility. Therefore, a much larger population had to be provided with basic utilities and services such as water, electricity and refuse collection.

We knew life was not an easy ride. It gave us incredible highs and desperate lows, when we least expected it. The phone call from my sister was one of those desperate lows; "Please come home as soon as possible. Dad is sick and it doesn't look like he's going to make it." My world collapsed. I could not picture my dear father dying in a hospital bed. He had been a good and caring father throughout his life and – the irony of fate – had just retired after a lifetime of hard work. "Will I've the courage to enter that hospital room? What am I going to say to him? Is it really the end of this earthly life for him?"

Once again, I said goodbye to Naledi and boarded a plane to Venice.

"I don't know how long I'll be away. You need to take care of yourself! But if my family will need me there for quite some time, I'll make sure you come visit me in Italy!"

"Your family, and your father in particular, come first. They desperately need you there!"

The moment I turned the corner of the hospital corridor and faced my father's room, I saw his face as he laid still, staring helplessly at the ceiling – but what really shocked me, was the whiteness of his hair, the grimace on his face and the pale colour of his skin, all signs of a person who was walking the last steps of his personal *'via crucis'* otherwise known as 'the way of the cross', as Jesus did before his crucifixion.

He was able to say a few words, words that I still carry with me; "*Non ci vedo chiaro*," - "I can't see clearly ahead of me." He knew he was dying. A few days later, a priest joined us for his Last Rites. "Maybe we'll meet again up there, Father. Go in peace and thank you for being a great person and for what you did for me and our family," I whispered to him.

He was gone.

His death rocked my world. With one foot in South Africa and the other in Italy, I lost perspective in life and felt confused. I was troubled by memories of the past - some precious and others I had to let go. I knew I had to refocus, regenerate my inner strength and think of a way forward. I also knew my family was not supportive of my relationship with Naledi, and I could no longer count on my father's wisdom to come to my rescue. I needed someone who understood me, and I booked Naledi on her first trip outside South Africa. She was joining me in Italy.

After a short stopover in Lisbon, the South African Airways flight landed in Milan, the Italian city of fashion and glamour. I told my mother and sister I needed to go on a "solo" trip to recover from my sorrow. Only my closest friends knew I was meeting Naledi, the love of my life. I vividly remember her joy as she exited the baggage collection area and found me waiting for her. She drank in the city like a child. Overwhelmed by the sight of classy people walking Milan's elegant streets, giggling as we sipped on aperitifs at typical Italian piazza bars close to the famous Duomo cathedral. This was worlds apart from the dusty roads of her village. I lost count of the "wow's" I heard from her whilst I drove my dad's car. From Milan to Geneva via Aosta, passing under the Mont Blanc tunnel, from Geneva to some small town in France, all the way to Paris. From there we continued to Strasburg, Munich,

Salzburg and finally back to Italy via Trieste, Florence, Rome, Urbino, Assisi, Bologna, Venice, Treviso and other small towns.

Now that I am in Treviso, close to my hometown, what do I do? Do I keep running away from my family because they will find it hard to accept Naledi? No! It is time for my family to understand that she is part of my life, and the only solution is for them to accept and respect my choice without being judgmental. Besides, I was tired of being made to feel like a fugitive in my own country, by my own family. So, one day, close to Naledi's trip back to South Africa, I decided to face them.

My mother and sister were probably wondering where I was and why I had never reached out to them during my "solo" trip. To prepare them, I asked one of my closest friends, a real master at conflict resolution, to let them know that I was on my way home in the company of Naledi and, in so doing, equip them psychologically in advance.

Naledi was anxious when I told her we were on our way to meet my family. "Will there be any drama because I'm with you?" she asked.

"We love one another and eventually they'll need to accept it. You'll be staying with my aunts, who are the kindest and most harmless people on earth," I reassured her. My aunts did not disappoint me: "Ah Elio, it's you! Ciao Naledi, you're very welcome, we heard everything about you and are so glad to finally meet you!" they greeted her.

"*Grazie*" - "Thank you", she uttered the only word she knew in Italian at that stage.

However, her real test was still ahead, with my mother and sister arriving soon.

As soon as my mother entered the room, she scolded me in the true Italian mama style. "Where have you been? Couldn't you let me know where you were?"

"Hello *mamma*, I'll tell you about my trip but first, I want you to meet Naledi, who came to visit us all the way from South Africa. I told you about my relationship with her."

Her attention shifted to Naledi. "*Buongiorno, come sta? Sono Bruna, piacere di incontrarla*," - "Hello how're you, Ms? I'm Bruna, pleased to meet you," she said very formally as she shook Naledi's hand. I knew my mother could be a bit difficult at times, but deep down I also knew she would eventually open up to Naledi. Her initial hostility came for the lack of exposure to people from other parts of the world, especially people with a different skin colour.

But my sister? An open-minded, well-travelled person? Would she let me down? I anxiously watched her face. "Hello Naledi, nice to see you again. It's been a while since I first saw you in South

Africa. This is an opportunity for us to get to know each other. Let me hug you as a warm welcome to our home."

The ice was finally broken. All that was needed was mutual love, respect and understanding – qualities that neither my family, nor Naledi were short of. I looked up and thanked my father for the help he provided from up above.

After spending some time at home, helping my family cope with the loss of my father, I made plans to return to South Africa. I began to feel like a foreigner in my own town and yearned to be under African skies again. It was painful to see my mother crying when I left. She knew she was going to face years of loneliness without a husband and a son to comfort her.

But now I was a true African...

New beginnings

The beast was dead, I realised when Nelson Mandela walked free on 11 February 1990, after spending 27 years imprisoned. To avoid an escalation of violence in the country and further international isolation, he was released unconditionally by the government of FW de Klerk, the last Apartheid president. The "terrorist" ANC and other political organisations were also unbanned.

Many Whites feared Mandela would turn his millions of loyal followers against them. Will Black people take revenge for the many years of oppression? Will South Africa fall into a state of civil war? Will it be a bloodbath?

This tall man, destined to be the country's first Black president, walked like a true leader out of the Victor Verster prison gates, accompanied by cries of "*Amandla! Awethu!*" - "The power is ours!" in isiZulu. He calmly addressed a massive crowd from the balcony of a parliamentary building with his very distinctive voice. The voice of someone who had not been broken after all those years of incarceration and still had an important mission to accomplish. Now released, his task was to see the birth of a new country with 'free and fair' elections for all its citizens.

Alea iacta est translates to "the die is cast". There was no turning back. He was needed to pave the way and avoid a bloody revolution in the process.

For Mandela to achieve his vision, he needed the close collaboration of other illuminated political, social and religious leaders and organisations. This was accomplished through intense negotiations that started with a National Peace Accord (NPA) in 1991, aimed at bringing an end to violence in South Africa and establishing a multi-party Democracy. The NPA was later consolidated into the multi-party Convention for a Democratic South Africa, known as CODESA 1 held in December 1991 & CODESA 2 in May 1992. The ANC and ruling National Party were the primary parties, plus parties such as the Democratic Party (DP), the South African Communist Party (SACP), the Inkhata Freedom Party (IFP) who later withdrew from the talks because of the exclusion of the Zulu King.

However, other parties boycotted the talks, such as the PAC and AZAPO on the far-left, and the Conservative Party (CP) and Herstigte Nasionale Party (HNP) on the far-right of the political spectrum. This caused concern for the split between those in full favour of a new South Africa and those who were against it, or harboured serious reservations.[18] Many people were involved in those negotiations, including Cyril Ramaphosa representing the ANC, and Roelf Meyer on the side of the NP. The ANC positioned itself as a key player in the negotiations to end Apartheid.

But as they say in the classics: "The natives were restless" – both Black and White.

In several townships, violence erupted between supporters of different parties, in particular the IFP with a predominantly Zulu membership and the ANC. The subsequent massacres showed there were forces hell-bent on destroying South Africa's chances of a positive outcome from the negotiations. There was talk of a "third force"; a group of secretive underground saboteurs with possible links to Apartheid agents, who were far-right, White suprematists. Organisations such as the Afrikaner Resistance Movement/Die Afrikaner Weerstandsbeweging (AWB) with sympathisers in state security forces, and elements within Black political and ethnic groups opposing the dominance of the ANC.

In the Sebokeng and Boipatong massacres of 1991 and 1992, over 70 people were killed. Following Boipatong, the ANC abandoned the CODESA 2 negotiations, accusing the White government of being complicit in the attacks.

The party launched countrywide mass action, which were the fuse for the Bisho massacre in 1992, where several supporters marching against the leadership of Ciskei, one of the Bantustans established by the Apartheid regime, were shot dead by soldiers.

An agreement was eventually reached, signed by de Klerk for the South African government; Nkosi *Sikelel' iAfrica. Ons vir jou Suid-Afrika. Morena boloka sechaba sa heso. May the Lord bless our country. Mudzimu. Fhatushedza Africa. Hosi katekisa Africa.*

South Africa was now a Democracy – but then, in 1993, Chris Hani, the general secretary of the SACP and former ANC and MK member, was gunned down in his driveway by a White right-winger. The radicalised Janusz Waluś, originally from Poland, was contracted to execute the killing. But an Afrikaans housewife, recognised Waluś and his vehicle and immediately called the police, leading to his arrest.

The intention was to disrupt the transition to Democracy and the peace negotiation process and bring the country to the brink of a civil war.

It almost succeeded. Millions of workers mobilised to commemorate Hani and riots erupted countrywide.

Mandela, though not yet president, addressed the nation on 14 April 1993, to call urgently for peace. His stature as a leader emerged in all its greatness at a time when the whole nation teetered on the brink of disaster. He appealed to all South Africans, Black and White, to stand together against those who, from any quarter, plotted to destroy the ideal of freedom and justice that many opponents of

Apartheid, like Hani, had fought for. "What an inspiration this man is! He could easily call for revenge, but he's clearly choosing the path of peace and reconciliation," I thought to myself.

The violence was quelled, but not our fears. Will it reach a boiling point again, when we will have no other option but to move back to Italy? Naledi and I tried to stay positive and have faith in this country.

"I'm sure we'll overcome all obstacles, heal all our pain from the past and find a way forward. We're blessed to have a great leader like Mandela," Naledi reminded me.

"I hope so, this is a great nation, rich in human and natural resources, with excellent infrastructure and growth prospects. If it could only find a way to turn the page peacefully, it would have the potential to progress even further. Besides, I invested many years of my life in this place and would be very sorry if my sacrifice and hard work were made in vain."

I was one of the many expatriates who had a plan B in a worst-case scenario. I could return to my hometown. Native South Africans, Black and White, had nowhere else to run to.

Many disillusioned local professional and skilled people who qualified to work abroad, looked for opportunities to start a new life elsewhere, predominantly in English-speaking countries such as England, Australia and New Zealand. Wealthy individuals and investors considered moving to countries such as Mauritius, only a four-hour flight from Joburg with a stable, tax-friendly financial environment. Joining the exodus were many long-standing European immigrants, going back "home", like the Sartor family.

The period of transition and uncertainty also impacted negatively on property sales, with houses being put on the market at much lower prices than their real value by owners who were in a hurry to leave South Africa. I am one of those who benefitted at the time, for I purchased my first apartment at a bargain from a gentleman who was emigrating to Australia.

I reminded myself of the story a rich businessman from Chicago told me during an executive protection detail: "I got rich when other people were abandoning the city centre during a period of crime, grime, fear and decline. They were leaving and I was investing!" In fact, at the time, some companies invested heavily in the then deteriorating Joburg CBD, acquiring properties at very low cost and refurbishing them with government incentives.

And me? I made up my mind to make South Africa my home. "This is where my heart and mind is. This is where I need to work hard to build my future."

***

My new country's big day finally arrived on 26 April 1994 when, on a gentle autumn day, about 20 million South Africans from all racial groups stood jubilantly in long and peaceful queues, patiently waiting to cast their vote for their party of choice. It was a time of celebration. A time in which South Africa truly became Desmond Tutu's Rainbow Nation.

"What a moment in history! I've been a witness to all sort of events in this country: discrimination and segregation, political strife, rioting, repression, bloody massacres, terrorism, criminality, negotiations, freedom – and now the very first democratic elections," I told Naledi while we were standing in one of those never-ending queues.

My excitement could not match Naledi's, though. She had been excluded all her life and made to feel as if she did not belong, as if she was less than a third class-citizen without any say in her country's future. But now, for the first time in her entire life, she could vote. She was "over the moon" when she dropped that folded piece of paper in the ballot box. That moment helped her heal. It made her forget what Apartheid had done to her, her family and her people.

"I suddenly feel free in my own country! I finally have a sense of belonging to this place. I know this day alone won't be enough for people to heal from the past. We'll need time to forgive those who have badly hurt us."

The ANC won with a resounding 62% of the vote, followed by the NP with just over 20% and the IFP with 10.5%.[19] The results paved the way to a government of national unity, with Mandela taking the oath as the first Black president of South Africa.

The nation was jubilant, everyone was dancing in the streets, including Naledi, who voted for the ANC "as a way to thank Mandela and his party for the sacrifices they had made during years of oppression."

"But I wonder how well they'll run the new South Africa, because there are big challenges ahead. Our people live in poor conditions. Too many of us have no jobs and still live in shanty towns. Life remains a daily struggle even if Apartheid is now dead," Naledi said.

"But for now I'm overwhelmed! You have no idea how it felt to be considered worthless throughout my life. To be humiliated and reminded of being of an inferior status in the country where I was born, where my ancestors are buried."

"Naledi, I despise all forms of injustice and I've always been supportive of those who happen to be victimised for the wrong reasons, be it for their physical aspect, handicap, religion, sex orientation or skin colour. But we know discrimination, bullying and harassment aren't going to disappear overnight. They'll always be present in society one way or another. People like us who believe in a just society, need to be united and keep fighting all forms of abuse."

Would South Africa be able to eventually turn the page on this senseless brutality? Great leaders, coupled with divine intervention, pulled us back from the brink of disaster and helped avoid a bloody civil war – but the future is still blurred.

There will be many more challenges ahead for this country, I thought to myself in one of many of my "me moments", that quiet time when I interrogate myself and search for my soul to give more meaning to my life.

This country has taught me harsh lessons through the diverse people I met. It helped me to grow into a better person and appreciate the precious things I, back home, had taken for granted: living in freedom in a just society, respectful of the rights and dignity of all its people.

South Africa has also given me my most treasured gift – love. Not only for this wonderful country, but also for a wonderful woman, who like the shining star her name implies, fought by my side to defy the Apartheid beast and allowed our love to flourish.

"You're a star, Naledi. I love you – forever."

Country of miracles

This is where my story ends – and starts – yet continues. I lived through events that inexorably shaped the future of South Africa, an amazing country at the far end of the African continent: my home.

I happened to be part of a tough time of South Africa's history, not only as a witness but also as a victim. I have experienced the impact of Apartheid on one's dignity, freedom and humanity, albeit not like Naledi, her family and her people. I, like her, refused to accept the *status quo*, and we defied it in our own peculiar way.

South Africa is now a very different country, with amazing potential, but still plagued by enormous challenges that must be tackled and overcome. The goal is for this beautiful country to be truly free; free from endemic poverty and unemployment; free from crime; free from corruption; free from inequalities; free from political incompetence. I am aware that no country can truly claim to be free from all of this, not even the most modern and advanced democracies, and I know that this view is rather idealistic; but thanks to its resilience, goodwill, resources and capabilities, I am confident that South Africa can strive to a much higher level of freedom and societal justice.

The road ahead is still steep and arduous, but this country has made miracles at its worst possible time in history. More will come, I am sure, so help her God!

Key pieces of Apartheid legislation mentioned in the book

- **Abolition of Influx Control Act of 1986** - The abolition of the Influx Control Act in South Africa was part of the broader dismantling of Apartheid-era laws. Influx control was a system designed to regulate the movement of Black South Africans into urban areas, primarily to maintain racial segregation and control the labour force. It had come into force with the Native (Urban Areas) Act of 1923.

- **Bantu Education Act of 1952** – It governed the education of Black South African (called Bantu by the country's government) children.

- **Group Areas Act of 1950** – It allowed the government to designate specific geographic areas for exclusive use by particular racial groups, primarily to enforce racial segregation.

- **Immorality Act of 1927 (amended in 1950)** – Initially enacted as the Immorality Act of 1927, it prohibited sexual relations between White and Black people. The act was later amended and expanded in 1950 as the Immorality Amendment Act to include prohibitions on sexual relations between White people and all non-White people, thereby reinforcing racial segregation and discrimination.

- **Pass Laws Act of 1952** – It required non-White individuals to carry documents, known as passes, to authorise their presence in restricted areas. The pass said which areas a person was allowed to move through or be in and if a person was found outside of these areas, he/she would be arrested.

- **Prohibition of Mixed Marriages Act of 1949** – It prohibited marriages between individuals of different racial classifications, specifically between White people and people of other races. This act aimed to maintain racial purity among the White population by legally enforcing racial segregation in marriage.

- **Publication and Entertainment Act of 1963** – it allowed the government to ban publications deemed "undesirable" for various reasons, including obscenity, moral harm, blasphemy, or anything considered prejudicial to the state's safety, welfare, peace, or order.

- **Reservation of Separate Amenities Act of 1953** – It legalised the racial segregation of public facilities, services, and amenities, such as parks, beaches, buses, and restrooms, designating them for exclusive use by specific racial groups.

- **Terrorism Act of 1967** – It allowed for the indefinite detention of individuals without trial if they were suspected of involvement in terrorism.

- **Unlawful Organisations Act of 1960** – It banned organisations that were deemed a threat to public order. Notably, the act was used to outlaw the African National Congress (ANC) and the Pan-Africanist Congress (PAC), both of which were key organizations in the struggle against Apartheid.

Source: Britannica https://www.britannica.com/

References

1. Wikipedia. "Dutch Reformed Church in South Africa (NGK)."https://en.wikipedia.org/wiki/Dutch_Reformed_C hurch_in_South_Africa_(NGK).
2. Wikipedia. "Putco." https://en.wikipedia.org/wiki/PUTCO.
3. G. Newham et al. 2006. "Diversity and transformation in the South African Police Service." Centre for the Study of Violence and Reconciliation. Johannesburg: Colorpress.
4. M. Swart. 2020. "Death on the 10th floor: The search for truth in South Africa." Al Jazeera. Available at: www.aljazeera.com/features/2020/4/20/death-on-the-10th-floor-the-search-for-truth-in-south-africa.
5. G. Newham et al. 2006. "Diversity and transformation in the South African Police Service." Centre for the Study of Violence and Reconciliation. Johannesburg: Colorpress.
6. Wikisource. "Terrorism Act, 1967." Available at: https://en.wikisource.org/wiki/Terrorism_Act,_1967.
7. A. Boddy-Evans. 2020. "Pass laws during apartheid." ThoughtCo. Available at: www.thoughtco.com/pass-laws-during-apartheid-43492.
8. Nuclear Threat Initiative (NTI). 2024. "South Africa – Country spotlight." www.nti.org/countries/south-africa/.
9. History.com Editors. 2010. Last updated May 30, 2024. "1902 The Boer War ends in South Africa." A&E Television Networks. Available at: www.history.com/this-day-in-history/the-boer-war-ends.
10. Maharaj, B. (Dr). 2023. "Indentured Indian labourers and their struggle for citizenship in South Africa." Daily Maverick, 15 November 2023. Available at: www.dailymaverick.co.za/opinionista/2023-11-15-indentured-indian-labourers-and-their-struggle-for-citizenship-in-south-africa/
11. Beale, M.A. 1998. "Apartheid and university education, 1948-1970." PHD Thesis. University of the Witwatersrand. Available at: core.ac.uk/download/pdf/188775743.pdf.

12. Albertus, R. W. & Tong, K. wai. 2019. "Decolonisation of institutional structures in South African universities: A critical perspective." Cogent Social Sciences, 5(1). Available at: doi.org/10.1080/23311886.2019.1620403.

13. African American Registry (AAR). Nd. "The Soweto uprising begins." www.aaregistry.org/story/the-soweto-uprising-begins/.

14. Dall, N. 2024. "I'm prepared to die: Mandela's speech which shook apartheid". Aljazeera. Available at: www.aljazeera.com/features/2024/4/20/i-am-prepared-to-die-when-mandela-shook-apartheid-changed-south-africa?_gl=1.

15. Chkoniya, L. 2023. "46 Years of Solitude: The Main Lessons of the Apartheid Sanctions Against South Africa." Reuters. Available at: valdaiclub.com/a/highlights/46-years-of-solitude/7.2023.

16. Liepollo Pheko, L. 2012. "100 years of Liberation Struggle – ANC, PAC and AZAPO – Between liberation and neoliberal politics." Kasa. Available at: www.kasa.de/fileadmin/user_upload/downloads/news/kasa/2012_03_07_pheko_100_years_of_liberation_struggle.pdf.

17. Liebenberg, D.C. Personal interview with an Afrikaner friend and colleague. Conducted on 10 August 2024.

18. SAHO – South African History Online, 2017. The Convention for a Democratic South Africa (CODESA): CODESA 1. www.sahistory.org.za/article/convention-democratic-south-africa-codesa-codesa-1.

19. The South African Editors. Nd. "South Africa's previous election results." Blue Sky Publications (Pty) Ltd. www.thesouthafrican.com/governmentpolitics/elections/.

Special thanks to SAHO (South African History Online) and Wikipedia

www.ingramcontent.com/pod-product-compliance
Lightning Source LLC
Chambersburg PA
CBHW051110030726
47504CB00006B/1874